The Dead Have Lots To Say

Twenty short stories set in Paris

Anna Redkina

DEDICATION

To Jérôme and Aliocha

CONTENTS

ACKNOWLEDGEMENTS

Jérôme Haupert, Silvia Ferreiro Sopeña, Aidan McNamara, Irina Gorshkova and Rebecca Lander for their help with this book and patience with the author!

Jojo, Julia, Lena, Luis, Nadia, Serge, Stephanie, Olivier, Roman... my dearest friends and my parents for their encouragement and patience with the author!

SECRET BLACK BOOK
4th arrondissement

The worst thing was the walking stick.

The doctors said that it was temporary, that the thigh would get better with time, but Yvonne knew that at seventy-four time rarely sorted things out. Arthritis it was, merciless and ugly, like the walking stick itself. She tried not to make a big deal out of it and joked about always having a free seat on the bus now.

"This is nothing," she kept telling her family and friends. "In fact, I can walk without it. This is just a back-up."

But it was always with her. It took her through Parisian streets, parks and gardens, museums and café terraces. It stayed near her bed, ready to help her get to the toilet, when her weakening bladder would wake her up in the middle of the night. It leaned on restaurant tables, and always got in the way when she wanted to grab a book from a shelf in her tiny Parisian flat.

On May 22, it faithfully led her to *La Place des Vosges*, Louis XIII Square - to the middle of it, to be exact - to her favourite bench, on the right from the main entrance. Yvonne loved sitting there, observing life unfold like a theatre play in front of her eyes, and no walking stick was going to change that.

"Out of sight, you, eye-sore!" Yvonne deftly hid the stick behind the bench.

The square was packed: families with children, youngsters with beers, boys with guitars, yogis, drunkards, readers, writers, dogs, cats, you name it. Just a few meters away a group of young girls were having a picnic on the lawn. They'd brought a red and white checked tablecloth and posh crystal glasses, which they kept filling with rosé champagne. The girls were giggling and chirping, feeding on big ripe strawberries as they drank. It had been unusually hot for the end of May, and they were wearing light summer dresses, blood red, sky blue, sun yellow. Stripes, dots and flowers showed firm breasts and strong thighs.

A soft voice distracted Yvonne. She turned her eyes from the girls and saw an old man standing near the bench and talking to himself.

"How come I never saw him approach?" Yvonne wondered. "As if he'd appeared out of thin air. I must be losing my hearing and eyesight too."

She listened. The old man was reciting poetry and doing it louder and louder. He looked weird, too. He was wearing an old-fashioned dark-green velvet jacket even though the thermometer hit thirty that afternoon. Yet, it fit his wide shoulders perfectly well, which was so unusual for his age. He must have been at least eighty, Yvonne thought, but he looked after himself, or somebody else did. His white beard was neatly trimmed, and he smelled of fine perfume, too.

How come she was the only one to notice him? He should have attracted attention by now, reciting in full voice, one hand on his belly, and the other dancing in the air, following the rhyme of a poem about love:

"Aimons toujours ! Aimons encore !..."

There was something touching about this old man. To encourage him somehow, Yvonne applauded:
"Bravo!"
He looked at her, surprised.
"Did you hear it?"
"Of course, I did. The whole square did, I think," and Yvonne showed a dimple on her right cheek. She always did when she smiled.
"You think so?"
Not really. She seemed to be the only one who reacted to this old man. How strange, she thought. At the same time, people are so self-absorbed nowadays!
"It is not every day that you hear somebody recite Victor Hugo's poems!" she winked.
"You recognized Victor Hugo's poem? How do you

know it was Hugo?"

"I used to be a teacher of French literature. It was part of the programme, of course, and one of my favourites."

The old man looked satisfied.

"Would you mind if I sit down?" He pointed at the bench.

"Of course, I don't mind; you have every *right* to sit on this bench. It's a public place, hence I don't own it. Fortunately, not everything is private in this country yet."

"Victor." the old man nodded, sitting down. "My name is Victor."

"Nice to meet you, Victor. Yvonne." She put her hand on her chest and slightly nodded too.

"So, what else did you teach, Yvonne?"

"Oh, plenty of wonderful authors! Balzac, Zola, Rimbaud..." she started to unfold her tiny fingers. "And then, more modern authors, for example..."

"Sorry," Victor touched her elbow. His touch was soft and somehow pleasant. "I meant, what else by Victor Hugo?"

"Oh, the biggest one was *Les Misérables*, of course."

"A real masterpiece, isn't it?"

"Yes, a real bestseller too! An epic work, a work of genius, subtle, admirable ... I just wish the author of this masterpiece hadn't been such a piece of crap, as it turns out he had been."

"What do you mean?"

"I read his biography a few months ago. A total

disappointment, you know. I couldn't even finish it, I was furious! His behaviour with women was disgusting!" She shook her head with disdain. "He was a hideous, horrible person."

"Really? Wasn't he the biggest romantic hero of all times?"

"No. A sexually obsessed, old paedophile!"

"A paedophile?"

"Seducing fourteen-year-old girls, how would you call it?"

"Many look and behave maturely enough at fourteen."

"What difference does it make?"

"Maybe they wanted him to? He was so desirable, rich and famous. What obstacle could age be to love? Love is blind, don't you think? So is passion."

"Those "love" experiences could be quite traumatising for a teenager."

"I'd agree with that, love can be painful, but it can happen at any age. And suffering is part of it. We don't live if we don't suffer, and love suffering is so bittersweet..."

He sighed, observing the picnic girls in front of them.

"He didn't seem to be the one who suffered, most of the time. He was quite amused, as some documents like *The Black Book* show it.

"And what do you know about *The Black Book*?"

"As an old man, Victor Hugo wrote his sexual conquests there. He invented some kind of code. "Swiss" meant he touched a maid's breast, for example. Oh, he loved touching maids, just like some other hero of our times! Apparently, Hugo associated Switzerland with cows, cows with milk, and milk with female breasts, the old pervert."

Victor seemed offended.

"On the contrary, a very clever code. Very creative."

"And when he managed to have sex with those poor maids," she continued without listening. "He'd write *"todo"* in Spanish, which means "everything". What a linguist, this Victor! What an inventive mind!"

Victor shrugged.

"Those word games were popular at his time. He proved himself very creative, that's all. As for those women... *Il y a des femmes qui prennent comme des allumettes..."*

Yvonne sighed and shook her head.

"Anyway," she continued after some silence. "I caught myself thinking that nowadays he'd never get away with what he did, like that Hollywood producer, remember? I mean, being so rich and famous, with such huge power... Remember Victor Hugo's death? All France was following his coffin. He was known for his progressive views, he was everywhere, in politics, *L'Académie française*, and he sold millions of copies of his books. Yet, he harassed women. We don't know if he literally raped his victims, although some of his biographies confirm it, and where to draw the line between "flirt", "favour" and "obligation..." But he did use women to satisfy his sexual appetite, and he did use his power and notoriety for that. He was very insisting, to say the least!" She exclaimed, fidgeting with her fingers as she always did in anger.

Victor didn't answer.

"Are you listening?"

He wasn't. He was enthralled by the strawberry girls in front of them. They were tipsy now and paid little attention to if their dresses showed too much of a thigh or a breast.

"Excuse me." Victor looked at Yvonne with a charming smile. "You know what it means to be old. You drift away sometimes. You were saying?"

You drifted away in a very certain direction, Yvonne thought. Another old pervert. Or, maybe, the same one? She looked attentively at his white beard, his old-fashioned jacket, and his small clever eyes.

"I was saying," she pulled herself together, "That Victor Hugo wouldn't get away with his behaviour with women nowadays, like all those Hollywood people."

"Hollywood people?" Victor asked, but the corner of his eye went straight under one of the girls' skirt.

"Take that Hollywood producer, for example. Remember, a few years ago? How did they call it in *Facebook*? Was it "Me also"? With a special typed sign in front? You see, like a square?" She drew a hashtag in the air. "You know, the campaign to denounce sexual harassment?"

Victor blinked.

"Sexual harassment. I guess it is easier for you to understand if I use Victor Hugo's "creative" code. It is when you do a "Swiss" or a "Todo" or you enter the maid's "Cave" without asking. Or touch her "Forest" for 2 francs. You get it?"

He nodded.

"Of course, he was an ardent defender of women's rights," Yvonne continued. "But real life proved stronger. It always proves stronger, doesn't it?" she observed Victor staring at the strawberry girls again.

"He was like most of them, Champagne socialists." She sighed. "They talk about respect and equality, and then before you know it they are sticking their dick into a hotel maid."

Victor blinked again.

"And the older he got the younger he liked them and more and more generous he became. Of course, all this money came from selling stories about poor Cosette..."

Yvonne's fingers were still twitching, and the horizontal wrinkles on her forehead looked deeper. But Victor continued in his nonchalant manner:

"Yes, he liked them young and beautiful - like any man would - don't you agree? He was not a second-hand bookseller when it came to love!" he chuckled, satisfied.

Yvonne stood up and took her stick from behind the bench.

"That's exactly what he used to say. Not a second-hand bookseller." And before Victor could say a word, she spiked her unsightly walking stick into his foot.

FELINOPHILIA
16th arrondissement

Sat 31 August
Charles B. is online

Charles B.
Where am I?
10:30

Enela E.
Who r u? Who added u?
10:31

Charles B.
I am Charles.
10.35

Enela E.
I don't know u. This must be a mistake.
10.36

Charles B.

Are you a cat?

10.38

Enela E. tries to block Charles B. but it doesn't work.

Charles B.

Are you a cat?

10.40

Charles B.

Are you a cat?

10.41

Charles B.

Are you a cat?

10.42

Enela E. tries to block Charles B. but fails again.

Enela E.

Why do u think I am a cat?

10.43

Charles B.

I can see a picture of a cat.

10.47

Enela E.
U mean, my profile picture?
10.48

Charles B.
I can see a blue cat.
10.50

Enela E.
This is my cat Yoda.
10.51

Charles B.
It is blue.
10.52

Enela E.
Well, yep, he's blue. Not going to paint my
cat green cause of his name, right?
10.52

Charles B.
What is so special about his name?
10.54

Enela E.
What drugs r you on?
10.54

Charles B.
Opium, mostly.
10.57

Enela E.
This explains some of it.
And where r u?
10.58

Charles B.
In Paris.
Rue du Dôme, Paris 16,
to be precise.
In a Clinique.
10.59

Enela E.
This explains most of it.
11.00

Charles B.
What world is this?
11.03

Enela E.
?
11.03

Charles B.
Are you human?
11.06

Enela E.
What else would I be?
11.06

Charles B.
Why do you pretend to be a cat?
11.07

Enela E.
I don't pretend to be anything.
And cats r cute.
11.07

Charles B.
Cute? That's the word you chose to
describe the most mysterious and
elegant creature in the Universe, only
possibly to be compared to a sphinx?
11.10

Enela E.
Typing...

Charles B.
« Ils prennent en songeant
les nobles attitudes
Des grands sphinx allongés
au fond des solitudes,
Qui semblent s'endormir
dans un rêve sans fin; »
11.17

Enela E.
I don't speak French
11.18

Charles B.
Pity
11.25

Enela E.
Who wrote it?
11.26

Charles B.
Me. I am a Poet.
11.30

Enela E.
Cool, but now people
r more interested in

kittens. Cute and funny.
11.31

Charles B.
Kittens are of no interest.
11.35

Enela E.
The Internet says otherwise.
They r soooooooo cool!
When I am sad or stressed,
I just watch videos of kittens.
Makes me feel better. Lol.
11.37

Charles B.
But what about real cats?
Don't you worship their
beauty and independence?
Don't you have this
Sensual satisfaction from
Smelling their fur and feeling
Their lithe little bodies
Underneath?
11.40

Enela E.
U r weird.

Charles B.
Typing...
11.40

Enela E.
There are some famous cats.
Like Grumpy cat. Hold on...
11.41

Charles B.
Grumpy cat?
11.42

Enela E.
Image sent
11.42

Charles B.
I have received the daguerreotype.
This cat looks bizarre.
11.45

Enela E.
It is so cute, but she died poor thing.
11.45

Charles B.

It resembles a human being,
Losing all of her mysterious
Feline Grace.
11.47

Enela E.

People liked her. She
had 2.4 million followers.
11.47

Charles B.

Followers where?
To the intellectual atrophy?
11.50

Enela E.

11.50

Charles B.

Cat's eyes are remote, mysterious,
inhuman, they contemplate me with the
same disdain as did my mistresses.
11.52

Enela E.
Charles B. and cats: adorable mix
11.52

Charles B.
What year is this?
11.53

Enela E.
?????!!!!!
11.54

Charles B.
Could you please tell me what year it is?
11.55

Enela E.
2019
11.55

Charles B.
I shall never be back here.
11.57

Enela E.
Why, weirdo?
11.57

Charles B.

It is a sad place with
Aesthetics of Cuteness.
11.59

Charles B. went offline.

SHORTS
18th arrondissement

Why the hell did she want to meet here?

Thibault spotted an empty table on the terrace near the entrance and headed there. At least he could sit outside.

He looked at his mobile phone only to find out that he was well in advance and he was running out of battery. Shit! To make matters worse, he was in one of the most touristic places in Paris. What proper Parisian meets his girlfriend at a café at La Place du Tertre? God, what's been wrong with her lately?

Now he has to wait on this lousy terrace drinking bad expensive beer and staring at mediocre artists and fussy tourists. Just look at their rucksacks with bottles of water sticking out of side pockets.

"What would you like, Sir?" He heard. "Would you like to have a look at our Happy Hour menu?"

"No, just *a demi*, please. Any lager." Thibault breathed out without looking at the waiter.

"No problem, Sir. Thanks for your order, Sir."

"The times have changed," Thibault thought. "Now the waiters are polite even in the most touristic places, and I bet he speaks English all day long."

"Please enjoy," his beer was served in seconds.

"Thank you." Thibault looked at the waiter.

A neat moustache was sitting on his full lips. His black beady eyes were smiling: "If you want something more sophisticated, please ask. I make incredible cocktails."

I hope to get out of here before that, Thibault thought, but replied politely: "Thank you."

He took his mobile out of his pocket and stared at the black dead screen for a second.

"She must be running late," he heard the calm, beautiful waiter's voice. "Just relax and enjoy this magnificent September evening. Could I possibly offer you another drink? A cocktail?"

"He's right." Thibault thought. "And it is The Happy Hour."

"Ok. Surprise me then." He said. "But nothing too strong, please, or too expensive."

"You are in good hands."

Thibault looked at the waiter's hands. They were very big. In fact, his whole body lacked proportions a little.

"How much are Happy Hour cocktails?" He checked.

"5"

"5?"

"5. See, ridiculously cheap." and he went inside.

Was he slightly limping?

"Today we start with A.M.B.A!" He reappeared and announced proudly, putting an elegant vintage glass in front of Thibault. It was decorated with a slice of lemon.

"My name is Henri," he introduced himself, sitting down next to Thibault. "May I join you for a while?"

Something didn't feel right. The terrace was full, but nobody seemed to care about Henri. As if he were to serve only Thibault. Also, his cocktail glass looked very different from other clients'. At the same time, most of them were drinking Coca Cola. Sad people. Thibault took a sip of his gorgeously presented cocktail. My, oh my, that was strong!

"Good? Do you like it?" Henri crossed his fingers.

"Strong." Thibault took a deep breath and a deep sip. "What's inside?"

"I am not going to give away all my secrets, am I?" Henri winked. "Let's say that there is a bit of Scotch. Also, some Rum, some Vermouth, the red one, you know. And maybe some Cointreau... Oh! I finally gave away all my secrets, didn't I?" He laughed. "And you haven't introduced yourself."

"Thibault."

"Do you come here often, Thibault?"

"Oh no, of course not! I *live* in Paris"

"Why don't you like it here?"

"Too touristy. I am not against tourists. I just don't like mass tourism."

He took another sip and moved closer to Henri.

"Look there. Do you see those?" He pointed at a group of tourists, mostly women.

"U-hum."

"You can say straightaway that they are American."

"Really? How?"

"They are extremely loud and they wear their typical shorts showing their ugly fat legs."

"Should they cover their ugly fat legs?"

"No, I didn't say that. But you can immediately see that they are not locals."

"You mean the French don't wear shorts?" And he quickly glanced at Thibault's checked Bermuda.

"Not this kind of shorts, no."

Thibault finished his drink and fretted:

"Do you know what time it is? My girlfriend should have been here by now."

Henri looked at his watch.

"Ten to seven."

"Twenty minutes late. This is so unlike her." He sighed and double-checked his mobile. It was dead.

"An excellent reason to have another cocktail, don't you think?" Henri clicked his fingers and ran inside only to reappear in a few minutes holding an intricate glass.

"*Et voilà!* Saratoga!"

Thibault observed his new friend for a few seconds.

"How come he is so short all of a sudden?" He looks like a dwarf. Has he shrunk?"

Then he looked at the promising Saratoga.

"Okey. Okeeey." Henri was singing. "I'll tell you.

Angustura, first of all. A few drops. I won't tell you exactly, to keep some of my secrets at least! Cognac liquor. Whiskey liquor. Noilly liquor."

Thibault desperately looked at his glass.

"All in a Bordeaux wine glass!" Henri added proudly. "Just try it! It is divine."

Thibault took a sip and nodded, gasping for some air.

"So, going back to the shorts," Henri said. "Do you mean that they have to wear the same shorts as French women do?"

"How can I explain ... Look, here is an example. When I travel, I try to live and look like a local. Last year when I went to Sri-Lanka, I bought local clothes. They are completely unlike anything we wear here in Europe. You know, men wear long dresses there, called sarongs. So, I bought one and was wearing it while I was travelling there."

"But you have blond hair."

"So what?"

"It is obvious that you are European."

"It doesn't matter. The locals see that I am making an effort to respect their culture."

"By wearing their traditional clothes?"

"Among other things. I eat like locals. I get up and go to bed like locals."

"U-hum."

"There is nothing worse when people travel and try to bring their culture with them."

"I still don't understand the connection with shorts..."

"Well, they would be more welcome if their clothes were more like French ones."

"Like, a beret and a striped shirt?"

"Henri, don't be silly! Not a beret, of course. This is a cliché. I am talking about normal clothes that correspond to proportions. Look at their big asses."

"So, it's about them being fat?"

"It's about them being Americans wherever they go. With their shorts and their Coke."

"But we are not going to drink Coke, are we? We will stick to another great American invention: Cocktails!" Henri winked. "It is high time for my Signature cocktail, my friend!"

"Could you bring me some water first?" Thibault begged.

"Why would you want water?"

"To survive your Cocktails."

"There is no way of surviving them, my friend."

"As long as there are no fizzy chemicals in them." Thibault shrugged.

Henri solemnly stood up. Another glass appeared in his hand, as if he were a magician.

"Dear Sir! Let me present you my Signature cocktail. Earthquake." He took off his hat and bowed.

Did he have a hat before?

Thibault bowed too.

What an amazing evening, he thought. Sometimes it is nice to improvise. Hopefully she is fine. It doesn't matter. What could have happened? Nothing. Nothing ever happens. I'll call her tomorrow. We always depend on technology nowadays. We used to survive without mobile phones. We used to meet in bars, in this country at least. Make new friends. So... fuck it.

"Are you still thinking about those American tourist asses?" Henri asked.

"Fuck it!" Thibault insisted loudly.

"Absolutely! Fuck it!"

"You know what, Henri. Thinking about it... They can wear whatever they fucking want. We are in a free world, although here it is a question of respect, not freedom, you know. But. But!" He raised his eyebrows. "But in this case they shouldn't be surprised that people see them as bloody tourists, don't like them or simply stare at them."

"Fair." Henri nodded, giving Thibault his cocktail.

"You call this Earthquake?" Thibault smelled the glass. Notes of Cognac? Brandy? No, Cognac. Pastis? Something with anisette. Strange colour, too.

"Your cocktail looks dodgy, Henri." He concluded. "But I will drink it, my friend."

"With great pleasure!" and he sent the whole of Henri's Signature directly into his stomach.

***

That was the last thing Thibault remembered.
He opened his eyes. It was morning.
He was in his room and in his bed.

Good.

Alone.

Good.

He was lying in his bed, under the covers, like a civilized human being.

Good.

He tried to get up, and groaned. A thousand hammers in his head started their sadistic concert.

His whole body was aching, too. Even his nails hurt.

"Courage!" He convinced himself and finally got up.

"I ran out of battery last night," Thibault remembered. "I need to check my messages."

He looked under the bed, and saw his phone.

Good.

There was something else there though, like a paper bag.

Thibault dragged the phone and the bag from under the bed.

"What is this?" He carefully examined the bag and pulled out a rolled art print.

"Did I buy it last night? I don't remember buying anything..." Thibault turned pale. "God, I didn't buy some art from La Place du Tertre, did I?"

"Courage!" He said to himself, and uncurled the print.

He studied it for a while, and then looked at the inscription at the bottom of it.

"You bastard! You are a grotesque genius little bastard, Henri."

And then he read the inscription again, out loud:

A Parisian looking at three fat American asses, by Henri de Toulouse-Lautrec.

WITNESSES
13th arrondissement

CHARACTERS

KRISTINA
Cleaner, illegal immigrant from Eastern Europe

PAULIE
Artist

REBECCA
Entrepreneur and mother of two

SOPHIE
In her eleventh year of a PHD in Sociology, living off the state.

VINCENT
Journalist

VINCENT: Thank you for coming.

REBECCA: Thank you for inviting us.

PAULIE: You are welcome.

KRISTINA *(with an accent):* You are welcome.

SOPHIE: Yeah. I hope this won't take long.

VINCENT: As you know, you are the four main witnesses of an extraordinary event that happened on April the 12th. I invited you here to put together your stories to write *The story* about Josephine Baker's recent appearance in Paris, for the newspaper which is...

PAULIE: Sorry, Vincent, just one detail: that woman *looked* like Josephine Baker. Josephine Baker died a long, long time ago. When was it that she danced in her banana skirt? In the 20s? The 30s?

SOPHIE: She died in the seventies. There is much more to Josephine Baker than a banana skirt.

PAULIE: Ok, but she is really dead.

(Makes a zombie face)

REBECCA: That woman looked *exactly* like Josephine Baker, though. I googled the pictures afterwards.

KRISTINA: Who is Josephine Bakery?

SOPHIE: The woman you saw near the Pitié Salpêtrière Hospital with a bunch of kids. It actually makes sense as she died in that hospital.

KRISTINA: The Negro woman?

REBECCA *(makes a choking sound):* How can you use this word?

SOPHIE: Can we start, please? I don't have much time; I have to hand in a new chapter of my thesis by Friday.

VINCENT *(cheerfully):* Let us start from the beginning, then! How exactly did she appear? Who would like to start?

SOPHIE: I will. I was walking past the hospital and I saw her. There she was, with her twelve kids. I didn't see any magical appearance, but the resemblance was striking.

VINCENT: Twelve kids? Did you count them?

SOPHIE: No, but she had adopted twelve kids and all of them seemed to be there.

PAULIE: Josephine Baker adopted twelve kids?

SOPHIE: Yes, when she stopped dancing in a banana skirt.

REBECCA: She then worked for the French resistance, during the war. She was a spy. She pinned notes into her undergarments knowing that no one would strip-search her as a celebrity. A truly remarkable woman. I googled it afterwards.

SOPHIE: And then she decided to show the world that people of any race and religion can live in peace. This is when she started to *collect* children. She went around the world to pick them: Japan, Algeria, Venezuela... And then she put them in one big house and exhibited them as her fighting-the-racism achievement.

VINCENT: So, you recognized the children and Josephine Baker?

SOPHIE: I didn't say that. I only said that the resemblance was striking.

REBECCA *(quietly):* Because it was her.

VINCENT: Could you describe her? What was she

wearing? What about the kids? What did they look like? How did they behave?

SOPHIE: She was wearing a long white dress and a hat with a huge feather, and...

REBECCA: Several feathers.

SOPHIE: I only remember one big feather. The kids looked bored.

REBECCA: Nonsense. They looked happy because they were going to the Zoo.

PAULIE: How the hell can you know that?

REBECCA: *Jardin des Plantes* Zoo is just around the corner. Where else would you take twelve kids?

PAULIE: If you say so.

SOPHIE: Actually, this could make sense, as the only place she ever took her poor kids was the zoo. I mean, when she was not exhibiting her "Rainbow Tribe" as she called them in her own Disney Land, for photos or advertising.

VINCENT: Please, let us put our judgments aside and move on with the story. Rebecca, you had mentioned a camera?

REBECCA: Yes, I was taking my kids to the nursery, but then I saw this amazing woman who looked familiar, so I couldn't help coming closer. She saw me, took a camera from her bag, and asked me to take a picture of her and her kids...

PAULIE: Yes, I was sitting in a café nearby, having a nice glass of Bourgogne Aligoté, and I saw her *(pointing at Rebecca)* take the picture. Actually, it was quite an interesting scene to watch. The woman who looked like Josephine Baker said: "Come on kids, come closer, show how much you love your mommy!" but the kids didn't seem very obedient. Two of them started to fight. "Brahim, *sale Arabe*!" I heard. It was one of the white boys.

REBECCA: This never happened! They happily posed for the photo with their mom. It was obvious how much they loved her and were grateful to her, poor creatures.

SOPHIE: Grateful for what exactly?

REBECCA: For adopting them, saving them from misery, and showing the world that people of different races and religions can live together in peace.

PAULIE: Yes, like that boy said: Brahim, let's live in peace.

REBECCA: For god's sake, he never said that. Vincent, who would you believe: a rough guy in his 40s who drinks his chilled Bourgogne Aligoté in the morning, or myself who was actually taking the picture?

VINCENT: Well, it is...

PAULIE: It was not chilled. You never drink Bourgogne Aligoté chilled.

SOPHIE: Bourgogne Aligoté?

VINCENT: It is very good with fish, chilled or not.

(Everybody becomes silent)

KRISTINA *(suddenly):* He say this. *Sale Arab.* I hear.

VINCENT (enthusiastically): Yes, Kristina, please, let us listen to your story.

KRISTINA: I hear this when Madame take photo.

Children very different. Arab, Negros, and Chinese *(pulls her eyes with her fingers to make them look Asian)*

REBECCA *(stands up):* My goodness!

KRISTINA: What? I nothing against, they look so.

PAULIE: This is so much fun!

(Takes out a notebook and starts drawing)

KRISTINA: Why this woman have all children? Not her children.

SOPHIE: To flatter her ego, mostly. She also set a trend. You know, now celebrities go to Africa to adopt babies.

PAULIE *(quietly):* I don't understand the idea of adoption as such. Kids are like farts: you can only love your own.

REBECCA *(to Sophie):* How can you bitch this incredible woman after what she did for this country and the world?

VINCENT: Please, let us go back to the story.

REBECCA: No, Vincent, let this pseudo intellectual answer.

SOPHIE: As Simone de Beauvoir said: "Being an intellectual is..."

PAULIE *diabolically laughs.* KRISTINA *yawns.*

REBECCA: You didn't answer my question.

SOPHIE: Have you looked at it from the kid's perspective? Being a tool for their mother's ego to prove something to the world? Those kids were unhappy and poorly looked after, didn't you google it *afterwards*?

REBECCA *shakes his head in disbelief.*

VINCENT: Please, ladies, let us go back to the story.

PAULIE: Ladies and a gentleman.

VINCENT *(apologetically):* Of course.

PAULIE: After Rebecca had taken the picture, the woman who looked like Josephine Baker put her camera away and started moving towards... ok, let it be *Jardin des Plantes.*

REBECCA: She gave me her autograph, and then headed to *Jardin des Plantes.*

PAULIE: I didn't see that.

SOPHIE: Then she suddenly stopped, looking at something. I looked in that direction.

VINCENT: Where was she looking?

PAULIE: There was a homeless woman, probably a refugee. She had four little kids with her.

SOPHIE: Five.

KRISTINA: Three.

REBECCA: All the children were crying.

SOPHIE: Not all of them. The baby was crying, but they always do, don't they? Others were playing.

REBECCA: The baby was cold and hungry, only a blind person couldn't notice that. Josephine couldn't just stand and look at this misery, so she came up to the homeless woman and asked her how she could help.

PAULIE: By that point I had finished my Bourgogne Aligoté, and came closer as I thought I could draw the scene. Josephine Baker - looking woman was talking to the refugee. She asked her if she could help her and her children, but I think the refugee didn't speak any French.

REBECCA: She spoke some French. She said: "Je ne

comprends pas", "Madame", and something else.

PAULIE: "Josephine" was trying to explain that she would like to take care of her baby, either as a God Mother or a Second Mother. She kept saying: the baby will have two mothers now...

REBECCA: Isn't it beautiful? She was doing what was the best for the poor baby...

PAULIE: Her Rainbow Tribe would be 13 now... Spooky!

(Makes a ghost face)

SOPHIE: But the poor woman could not understand Josephine and *(imitates Rebecca)* "what was the best for her poor baby". So, Josephine started to use gestures and mime to explain herself. She reached out and took the baby from her arms.

REBECCA: She didn't. She only pointed at the baby.

SOPHIE: She bloody did. Why else would the poor refugee start screaming?

REBECCA: But Josephine's intentions were good.

SOPHIE: I never said the contrary. It always starts with good intentions.

PAULIE: That was quite a scene. I drew it.

Shows a drawing of two angry women and children around them.

SOPHIE: It was complete chaos: the homeless woman screaming, children crying, running everywhere, until somebody called the police.

VINCENT: Who called the police?

SOPHIE: I don't know. It was somebody from the

neighbourhood, perhaps.

REBECCA: That was ridiculous as Josephine gave the baby back to the woman, kissed her, gave her some money and managed to explain that she would take them all to the zoo. But the Police arrived too fast...

SOPHIE: Josephine finally let the baby go and called the mother Imbecile.

PAULIE: She never insulted the refugee. She just angrily gave the baby back, and walked away. They didn't walk away together.

REBECCA: They did!

SOPHIE: In any case, the Police arrived.

KRISTINA: When I hear word police, I run away. But homeless woman happy with her baby and understand nothing.

REBECCA: The police took them both to the station.

SOPHIE: No, they didn't even pay attention to Josephine, and only took the refugee and her children.

PAULIE: The woman who looked like Josephine tried to negotiate with the police, saying that it was all her fault, but they didn't listen. Then she just disappeared into thin air with all her kids.

SOPHIE: I am sure the refugee is already on her way to her country facing war and misery again.

VINCENT: The police say that they never saw anybody like Josephine Baker when they arrived. And they would have remembered twelve children of different backgrounds.

KRISTINA *(scoffs)*: I believe my eyes!

REBECCA: I saw what I saw. The police are lying.
SOPHIE: Of course they are.
PAULIE *(finishing his drawing):* Without a doubt.

THE IRON LADY
7th arrondissement

(Translated from French)

"La tête de l'Armée!"

My last words got lost in the Kingdom of the Dead.
Almost two hundred years have passed like a blink.

***

I opened my eyes and sat up on my red quartzite tomb. Bright as always, I quickly realised what was going on.

I simply rose from the dead, Glorious and Great as ever; my tomb was right in the middle of the marvellous Dome of The *Invalides*.

An excellent idea to bring my remains here, I agreed.

Pleased that France still remembered Her True Heroes, I jumped on the ground, stretched my legs and looked around. I saw a lot of people wandering about the

Invalides, admiring the vaults and statues, reading about my Glory. A pleasant scene to see indeed!

The most loyal of them were even wearing a Bicorn made of paper. Was it still fashionable or was it another sign of memory and admiration of my War Genius? A lot of boys were wearing it and this filled me with pride: future generations were being brought up as real men and true solders!

I was an example to them, and the Laurels on my head were light and easy to carry, just like it had been for Caesar.

Centuries later Fortune and Honour still marched beside me!

I couldn't wait to see what my country and its capital had become, so I marched to the exit. I also needed to verify something very important for the city of Paris and France itself.

I walked out of my magnificent home and turned to the left; passed the canons that reminded me of Our Glorious Battles, and went straight on to *Rue de Grenelle*.

Paris was majestic as always. It was a warm May day, streets were clean and wide; I noticed a bizarre way of transportation and some shameless fashion, of course, but apart from that Paris was as triumphant as it was in my days.

On the crossroads with *Avenue de la Bourdonnais* I turned right and continued to walk until a few meters later I stopped and froze in disbelief. Right in front of me there was a gigantic Iron Tower, ripping the beauty of Paris and its very Sky. I naively hoped it was just a spectre, but closing and opening my eyes several times didn't make it go away: it was still there, like a rusty pipe rising in hideous contrast to the white Parisian buildings.

Although filled with disgust, I still wanted to find out the truth about this rusty chimney, so I went in its direction.

Another suspicious thing was that the closer I was getting to it, the more obviously I could hear the barking languages of our enemies, particularly the one of the islanders from across the channel.

They were swarming like flies underneath that Iron Tower.

Who was buried in this giant, uglier than the Devil himself and higher than the Pyramids in Egypt? An emperor, a general, a hero? Why so many people? I had to admit that their number largely exceeded the number of my "guests" at the *Invalides*.

How insulting!

Overwhelmed, I observed a sign welcoming *visitors*. Visitors? What do they mean by *visitors*? Thank goodness, the French language came first, but it was followed by the language of those cowardly oligarchs from The Foggy Albion, our worst enemies and the ardent haters of our Dear *République*; I was sure that two hundred years later they still worshipped their Kings and Queens! I was furious; even more so when I saw the inelegant Cyrillic letters, and those cold-loving peasants were now welcome too?

O tempora, o mores!

I had to find out why all those people were there.

"Mademoiselle!" I asked a petite woman with pretty curls.

She just shrugged and said something in her language.

I knew very well the language of that enervated, superstitious, *pantalon* nation incapable of anything worthy.

They were here, too! What happened to my *Patrie*?

I wandered around trying to find somebody who spoke French, but finally I had no other choice than to ask one of the *visitors*.

My numerous English lessons with Count Lascases finally proved useful.

"*Excusez-me, sir*," I asked a young man. "*Who buried here?*"

He didn't say anything, just blinked.

I repeated.

"*Please say me who buried in the Tower?*

"What, this?" He vaguely waved at the rusty monster.

"Yes, this Iron..."

"Iron Lady?" The man smiled.

"*Iron Lady, yes!*" I was becoming impatient. "*Juste tell me who buried there?*"

"Nobody is buried there. It is the Eiffel Tower, weirdo."

And he walked away.

"Weirdo?"

Count Lascases clearly didn't teach me that word!

This conversation only intensified my suspicions. I was sure those intriguing and enterprising islanders were at the heart of it and plotting something with other nations against France, like they have always done. Or maybe they were standing all alone against everybody now?

I noticed most of them were going up and down the Tower, some in cabins, some on foot. I didn't trust those devilish cabins and moreover I was used to long and exhausting campaigns so a few flights of stairs didn't scare me.

Gifted with an excellent *physique*, I almost flew up to the top of the Tower and the overwhelming view of all Paris took my breath away.

With my eyes of an eagle, I distinguished all the Monuments of Paris, one by one, and then I saw the one I was looking for. When I left this world, it was only a concept, *my concept and my project,* and now it was there, even more beautiful than I'd ever imagined. They did finish it! They did finish the Arch in the memory and the Glory of our Soldiers, our Men, our Hopes and Victories. They did finish my *Arch of Triumph.*

Tears of pride and joy filled my eyes: France was Great, She...

"Excuse me!" I heard the barbaric language and felt

somebody's hand on my shoulder.

I turned around.

"Could you take a photo of me, mate?"

A photo? Mate? He was holding a strange looking object.

I knew it was a provocation, and it only confirmed my theory of them plotting. I had to put together a strategic plan of how to fight this silent invasion, and being an outstanding strategist I would definitely not rush things. I was going to save France and its ideals of *République* in due course. Meanwhile, I just looked at the *rosbif* with disdain, pretended I didn't understand English, and turned away to contemplate the beauty of my Country.

SUPER, SUPER COOL!
3rd arrondissement

"Alice, where are we?" Gertrude grabbed my hand. Hers was firm and humid. She must be scared, I thought.

I looked around. It was certainly a change from our recent place: we were back to Paris. Real Paris. We had just appeared sitting in the middle of the street. *Rue de Chapon*, I read on the building in front of us, *3e arrondissement.*

"I think we are back in Paris, my love."

Gertrude let go of my hand, stood up and stretched her legs. I was still sitting on the ground, slightly out of breath.

"Come on!" Gertrude said, regaining control. "Get up, Wifey!"

I'd been dead for fifty-four years, but I found it quite easy to get back on my feet.

"Easy-peasy!" I said.

"How do you feel walking after all this time?" I asked Gertrude.

"Never been better."

And then something even more incredible happened. Our lovely white poodle Basket appeared right in front of us. Just like that!

"Basket, my big boy!" Gertrude called out his name through tears.

Basket jumped into her arms, then mine, then he jumped back down and started to dance in circles around us as he always did in joy and gratitude, then he barked, and then he even peed himself a little.

Gertrude kept stroking Basket and saying:

"Where have you been, big boy, huh? Where have you been all this time? I guess nobody has been giving you daily sulphur baths over there." She sighed, examining his hair. Then she looked at his teeth. "Your toothbrush was lost in eternity, too, from what I can see!"

I actually found him looking quite well, given the circumstances, but I didn't want to argue. The most important thing was that the three of us were reunited here in Paris.

I took Gertrude's hand and we set off for one of those carefree rambles like we used to do when we were alive.

"Paris hasn't changed that much, don't you think?" I squeezed Gertrude's hand.

"Have you seen the number of art galleries in this part of town?" Her eyes were restless. "I wonder what they are worth."

I would rather just walk with her and Basket the whole of eternity, but I knew that once Gertrude had something in her head there was no way of getting it out.

Just at that moment we were walking past an art gallery.

"Concept Gallery," I read. "Shall we go and have a look, my love? Maybe you'll discover a new Picasso?"

"I doubt it, Wifey," Gertrude said. "But let's have a quick look."

I knew she was pleased.

We entered a cosy hall with a few people talking and laughing, and two guys sitting at a small table.

"Good morning, *Mesdames!*" they stood up immediately and hurried to welcome us.

They were brothers. They were not identical twins, but they spoke in unison, smiled in unison, even breathed in unison. They must have shared the womb, I thought, even though physically they were quite different. Both had a little piece of plastic pinned to their shirts: "Jean, Art Consultant" and "Jacques, Art Consultant".

"Art consultant, huh?" Gertrude smiled.

Basket barked joyfully.

"He is a very peaceful and friendly dog." I reassured Jean who became a little pale.

"So, *Mesdames!*" Jacques continued, smiling. "Would you like to visit our art gallery? We have an incredible Art Event going on right now. An internationally acclaimed artist from England, *Darren Dove*, presents a concept of an interactive exhibition among other things."

"A must see." Jean solemnly nodded, putting his hands into the pockets.

"Super, super cool stuff."

"There are two exhibition rooms." Jean invited us to follow him. "I will leave you alone in the first one: it is a classic exhibition with a few objects, and the concepts are explained quite clearly on the wall. But the second room is special, and I will accompany you on this amazing journey through human diversity."

"Human diversity?" Gertrude knitted her brows.

"Everything in its own good time." Jean laughed and winked at Gertrude, and then at me. Then he hesitated for a moment and winked at Basket, too.

"Super cool!" Jacques approved.

We were standing in the middle of a big exhibition room.

"Enjoy, *Mesdames*!" The brothers left us to enjoy the promising *Darren Dove*.

Gertrude always had a soft spot for the English, after the Spaniards and the Russians, of course.

"Let's see what this genius Darren is all about, Baby Precious."

The first Art Object was simple: it was a brown ball in a glass box.

"Victory." I read underneath.

"Victory." Gertrude echoed. "What the fuck is this?"

"Victory." I shrugged.

"The ball is ugly." I added.

The next object was more elaborate; it was a silver skull looking at a round mirror. It was called "Time". Basket barked.

"I like this one too, big boy." Gertrude nodded. "It makes some sense at least."

Gertrude approached the skull, and looked at the mirror too. Now Gertrude and the skull were looking at me from the mirror.

That gave me goose bumps, even though this could sound weird, given that I was already dead.

"Gertrude," I said. "Let's move on."

We then bumped into a blue plastic horse, lying on its side.

"Death," I read on the wall behind it.

"Death of what?" I asked Gertrude.

"How the heck would I know, Wifey?" She scoffed. "Death of Art, probably?"

"How are you doing, *Mesdames*?" I heard Jacques behind my back. "I bet you are enjoying every bit of it?"

"To be honest, I am puzzled." Gertrude said, leading him to the next object. There were three dots and a vertical line between them, chaotically drawn on a pink canvas.

"What the hell is this?"

"A concept of a portrait."

"A portrait of a portrait of a portrait of a portrait?"

"Wow! You really got it!"

"Super clever stuff, huh!" Jean also appeared from nowhere.

"But there is nothing in here. Just a few spots."

"Hidden is more important than obvious, Madam."

"Really?"

"Conceptual Art, Madam."

I remembered when Picasso painted Gertrude's portrait, but many found little resemblance to her. He then said: "She will eventually look like her portrait." I found those words so beautiful. I was sure Gertrude was thinking of it, too. I saw how those ugly dots and lines were making her sad.

"Let's go to see the main part!" I suggested. "The inter..."

".... active!" the brothers lifted their thumbs in unison.

"Let's discover this little treasure indeed!" Jacques said with a conspiratorial wink. "Follow us, *Mesdames!*"

We found ourselves in a spacious room with a tree in the middle. It was made of pieces of cardboard, wood and fabric, and its branches were covered with socks, like dead leaves. There were hundreds of socks, hanging from the tree, socks of different colours and sizes.

"*The Tree Of Life, by Darren Dove!*" Jean announced. "Come. Come closer, *Mesdames!*"

We came closer. Basket started running around the tree, sniffing for something.

"A Real Art Critic!" Jacques laughed.

I had a closer look at the socks. There were cotton, silk, woollen, lace ones, striped and checked, plain and patterned, new and old, and even some with holes. Some smelly ones, too.

"Diversity!" Jean said proudly.

"Diversity?" Gertrude was observing a rainbow sock.

"This tree represents human diversity." Jean nodded.

"And exchange." Jacques added.

"And exchange. Of course."

"The idea is that you leave one of your socks and take somebody else's with you. This way you create a connection with another human being and take home an Art Object! Well, a part of it."

"Clever, huh?" Jean said.

"So, what do we have to do?" I asked.

"Could you please take off one of your socks?"

I looked at my feet. Then at Gertrude's. Then at mine again. I was wearing simple white socks, but Gertrude's were heavy brown stockings.

"Would those do?" I asked the brothers.

"They are super cool." Jacques approved.

"Vintage." Jean nodded.

I was wondering how Gertrude would react, as she hadn't said a word so far. That was very unlike her. Her eyes were following Basket, who was still running around the tree. She was thinking about something.

"Gertrude," I said. "What should we do?"

"Be brave and cool, *Mesdames!*" Jean laughed. "Take off your socks."

"But first, choose your new sock from the tree." Jacques suggested.

Gertrude was still holding the rainbow sock.

"This one is super cool." Jacques approved.

I pointed at a striped blue sock next to it.

"Great choice." Jean nodded.

I took my right sock off, then put on the new one, and Gertrude did the same. The brothers applauded.

"Now you have your first Art Object for free."

"Indeed!" Gertrude said.

"Basket!" she called. "Let's go!"

"How did you find the concept?" Jean asked.

"Fresh!" Gertrude petted Basket's head.

She was up to something, I could tell.

The brothers gave each of us a brochure: "Here you go, *Mesdames.* You will find more information about our gallery, sponsorship and our future projects. A lot of cool stuff is yet to come!"

We thanked the brothers and left the exhibition.

"For Christ sake!" I said. "That was weird."

Gertrude didn't say anything.

"Why are you not saying anything? I saw you there, all silent, no sarcastic comments, exchanging socks, like an imbecile."

Gertrude kept silent, smiling.

"Now, look at you, Matisse and Picasso's friend, the Great Gertrude Stein, going back to eternity in a stupid rainbow sock!"

Gertrude burst into laughter. I adored this laughter: so naughty, so real, so loud!

"Did you see Basket in there?" she asked.

"I did. He was up to something, too." I started to be a bit annoyed as they teamed up excluding me like they did sometimes.

"He was up to something, indeed." Gertrude took my hand, still laughing. "He pooped under the *Tree Of Life*, dear Alice, I saw it! Right on its deep conceptual roots! Right in the middle, Wifey, right in the middle!"

MOLIERE FOUNTAIN
10th arrondissement

Ladies and Gentlemen, welcome to Paris. Our Eurostar train is arriving at Gare du Nord. Please accept our apologies once again for this delay ...

Kate looked at her watch.

1 a.m.

"Excuse me," she asked a red-cheeked guy by the exit door. He looked Parisian. "Do you think I will be able to get the tube at this time of night?"

"If you are lucky," the red-cheeked guy said mysteriously and impatiently pushed the OPEN DOOR button. He kept pushing it until the train stopped and the door opened.

"That was helpful!" Kate got off the train, pulling her suitcase down and unfolding the handle. She looked at her watch again.

1.10 a.m.

"I don't think I want to push my luck," she murmured

and followed the TAXI sign.

"The corner of Rue Richelieu and Rue Moliere, please." She told a middle-aged taxi driver with round glasses and a funny goatee.

"Of course, Miss." He opened the rear door for her and deftly put her suitcase into the boot. "I know this corner very well. We will be there in no time."

There was no traffic at this time of night, so they quickly left the *Gare du Nord* area and were gently moving southwest. It was unusually warm for March. Kate opened the window and took off her scarf. The weather forecast had promised at least fifteen degrees less.

"Was your train late?" The driver asked, adjusting his glasses.

"One and a half hours!"

"Oh, my, oh my! Is it your first time in Paris?"

"It is. My sister has just moved here, so here I am! Can you imagine, I am twenty-two and I've never been to Paris before!"

Kate looked at the window. The city looked so calm, so peaceful, and so majestic at night. She already started to like it. The only unusual thing was that she didn't see any people. It was very late, true, but the streets were *totally* deserted. There were lights in some windows, and even some cafes and restaurants seemed open, but she didn't see a single soul. The air smelled of croissants, which was also unexpected at that time of night. The city seemed too perfect, as if she were in a film about Paris, or a postcard, but not Paris itself. Weird.

"Twenty-two!" The driver laughed, and quickly looked at Kate in the rear-view mirror. "Everything is ahead of you at twenty-two, including Paris. And you are lucky to be able to see your sister whenever you want. You catch a train on the other side of the tunnel and voilà! I never got to see my brother Mikhail since I moved here. I emigrated after the revolution, but he never managed to come to Paris to visit me."

"After the revolution?"

"Yes, the Russian Revolution."

What the hell is he talking about?

"It was a long time ago," the taxi driver agreed, smiling and stroking his neatly trimmed goatee. "My name is Ivan Afanasyevich, by the way. You can call me Ivan."

"Kate."

"That's a beautiful name." Ivan said. "So, tell me, Kate, does your sister like Paris?"

"She ab-so-lute-ly loves it! She has a nice apartment, which is apparently tiny, but it is part of Parisian life, I heard. She loves her job, and her French boyfriend, of course!" Kate blushed.

"Ah, she is like my brother Nikolai, then! I have two brothers Nikolai and Mikhail, you see. Mikhail dreamed of Paris all his life and never got here. Nikolai lived in Paris, and he absolutely loved it. I have lived here most of my life, but never felt the same way."

"Why?"

"Nikolai was a scientist, and even though at the beginning his life here was hard, little by little he got proper recognition from the scientific community. He had Parisian friends. However, I've always had it difficult. I had two badly paid jobs, and just worked day and night. When I didn't work, I tried to write poetry. I sent it once to my brother Mikhail, but he said that it was too dark, all gloom and doom and "shamelessly autobiographic". So, I played balalaika and drove my taxi. I played in a Russian restaurant; hence I mostly spoke with Russian people. But I missed my family and especially my brother Mikhail."

"Why couldn't you see your brother Mikhail?"

"We were in our twenties when I left Moscow for Paris. Mikhail stayed, because he couldn't imagine how a Russian writer could live without his Motherland at the time."

"Your brother was a writer?"

"Yes, he wrote short stories, novels and plays. He became very famous after he died. Have you read "The Master and Margarita?"

Kate shook her head. "It rings a bell, though."

"It became a cult book in Russia in the 80s, but international critics also consider it one of the best one hundred books ever written."

"But back to the story," Ivan continued. "As Mikhail's books were satirical, and his sharp humour didn't spare anything, including the Great Russian Revolution, his novels were not published, and his plays were rejected by most theatres. He asked the Soviet Authorities to give him a permission to leave the country to go to Paris. O, he dreamed of Paris! He asked me in his letters to go to some sites, and to make a full description of them, as if photos were not enough! When he was working on his play "Moliere" he asked me and Nikolai to go to the Moliere Fountain and write in detail about the material and colour of the Moliere statue, of the figures of the women at the base, whether water still ran in the fountain... He had built his own Paris in his imagination. He lived in a 17th century Parisian fairy-tale... He was dying to visit it, and, most importantly, to visit us, his brothers, meet his nephews and nieces... At the beginning he asked for a two-week permit, but then, as his situation in Moscow was getting worse, he asked them to let him leave for good, since his country didn't seem to need him as a writer. He ended up writing directly to Stalin."

"To Stalin?"

"Yes, you know, Joseph Stalin."

"But that was a long time ago, wasn't it? "

"Yes, it was in the thirties." Ivan said firmly.

What a freak!

He sounded so convinced, though, that Kate decided not to argue. Who cares if the story is a true one, as long as we want to know what happens next?

"Did Stalin reply?"

"Stalin called him personally! Stalin, by the way, saw one of Mikhail's plays seventeen times, and then all of a sudden the play was banned. Anyway, Stalin called. He asked my brother: 'Do you really want to leave?' 'Not if I can work in my own country', Mikhail answered. OK, Stalin said and hung up. The next day, a few theatres called Mikhail offering to stage his plays. Like by magic! Mikhail was so happy! He now had a hope that the government would give him a two-week permit to come and visit us, too. He applied straight away. A refusal. He thought it was a mistake, and applied again. Another refusal. He kept applying, but in vain.

After a few months of success, he started to get refusals from theatres, too. He decided to write to Stalin one more time, but this time there was no answer. He wrote again and again, he was desperate. Silence."

"Why?"

"Stalin was unpredictable. He liked to play with people. He was moody. There could have been thousands of reasons."

"What happened to your brother?"

"He lived in Moscow in extreme poverty, without any work or recognition, writing his masterpiece "The Master and Margarita" which was to become one of the most praised books in the history of literature, but he never got to know any success. He died from a kidney disease at the age of 49. We wrote to each other until his death, though. I sent him some money whenever I could, and it helped him and his wife get by. I kept sending him my poetry, too, but he never said anything about it again. I followed his advice and made it less "gloom and doom", but he never said a word. I didn't insist, and then he was dead. So, I will never know what he thought of my recent poems."

"Could you not go back to Moscow to see him?"

"Impossible. I was... let's call it a political refugee. They would kill me if I went back. You see, things were quite tough back in the thirties."

"What a sad story..."

"It is indeed. But no need for sadness as we are arriving at your destination and you will see *your* sister very soon." Ivan scratched his goatee cheerfully. "Time goes fast with a good story, doesn't it? Here it is: the corner of Rue Richelieu and Rue Moliere, young lady!"

"Thank you, Ivan." Kate opened her purse. "How much do I..."

At that moment the front door suddenly opened, and a Black Cat of unimaginable proportions got inside and sat next to Ivan.

Kate wasn't able to finish her sentence.

The Cat carefully closed the door and said:

"Good evening!"

Then he bowed and gave his paw to Ivan.

"Let me introduce myself..."

Kate, astonished, noticed a bottle of champagne in the Cat's other paw. She pinched her arm a couple of times. Ouch! She was not dreaming.

"Behemoth, for Christ sake!" the door opened again, and Kate saw a good-looking man with a pince-nez.

"Behemoth, get out of here!"

"Excuse me, Master!" Behemoth got out of the car

and theatrically helped the man get in. "I just wanted to *faire ma connaissance* with your brother!"

Ivan didn't move, as though he were in a trance.

Then his goatee and his lips started to tremble.

"Behemoth... Master... How come...?"

He was staring at the steering wheel, unable to look at the Pince-Nez Man, whom the naughty Cat was calling his brother.

Finally, tears broke out of his eyes; big, heavy tears, leaping onto his clothes.

Ivan turned his head and touched the Pince-Nez Man's face.

"Mikhail." He said quietly. "I recognized your voice immediately, you see? No matter how many years have passed..."

And he fell into his brother's arms, sobbing.

Tears started to well up in Kate's eyes, too, but she pulled herself together and said loudly:

"Wait a moment, gentlemen. What is going on here? You are supposed to be dead in the 30s." she bent forward and gently poked Mikhail. "And who is this huge French-speaking Cat?"

"Not only French speaking!" she heard Behemoth's mewling voice. He sat next to her and started to unfold his claws.

"I also speak English, Spanish, quite decent Chinese, Russian as I was born in this vast and rather mysterious country, some Japanese, too..."

"Behemoth, stop it! You do not speak Japanese!"

Mikhail turned his head, still holding sobbing Ivan in his arms. "I am sorry, Miss, for him and for this unusual scene that you have to witness."

"It is a strong scene, but what is..."

"Champagne?" Behemoth interrupted, raising the bottle.

"I would also like to thank you, Miss, for bringing my brother directly to me. I don't know if it was a pure coincidence, but here he is. Moreover, I do not believe in pure coincidences. If you knew how much time I spent chasing him. I know Paris "like my five fingers" now, as we say it in Russian. A fascinating city, I must say, *exactly* how I had imagined it, by the way! Ivan, why do you never come to Moliere Fountain? It would have been so much easier to find you. But never mind. Miss..." – his eyebrows raised-

"Kate"

"Miss Kate here brought you to me. Thank you, Kate. Thank you so much again. I absolutely needed to see my brother to talk about these among other things." He took a pile of paper from his pocket.

"Manuscripts!" he shook them with satisfaction.

"Manuscripts don't burn, as you know!" Behemoth lit a cigarette.

"For Christ sake, Behemoth! You see, my friends, I was allowed to take one of my characters with me. I chose Behemoth because I thought we needed some fun. See all the fun we are having now..."

"I only quoted you, Master!"

"What manuscripts?" Ivan turned pale.

"Your poems, stupid! I took them with me too, as I never answered you and I have a lot to say!"

"This champagne is wasted, gentlemen. It is warm. Too many tears, not enough joy and celebration, if you ask me."

"Nobody asks you, Behemoth! And let's get out of this car, don't you think it's time to get out of this car *for good*, Ivan?"

Kate's head spun, and she felt something in her hand. It was her suitcase handle.

She was sitting in the middle of the road. The car was not there anymore. Ivan, Mikhail and Behemoth's silhouettes were fading away on the horizon.

Kate got up and approached the fountain. The water was still running from the lion's mouths, but she already knew that it would stop in a few minutes.

A homeless guy appeared from nowhere; he was sleeping cuddling a bottle of rosé, with a childish smile on his face. There were a few old books by his side. Was he going to read them or sell them? Another book was lying on the fountain border next to an empty beer can. "Balzac," Kate read. "*La Peau De Chagrin*".

She also saw a few people passing by. Actually, Paris was quite busy even at night.

The temperature dropped drastically and matched the pessimistic forecast.

Kate was trembling.

She put on her scarf and dialled her sister's number.

Jenny was mad.

"Where have you been? I've been worried sick! I've tried to call you a million times, but I kept getting some static silence."

"I don't know where I have been *exactly*, Jenny, although I guess I was somehow let into Mikhail Boulgakov's Paradise."

She started to cry.

"You are out of your mind. Where the hell are you now?"

"The corner of Rue Richelieu and Rue Moliere, near the Moliere Fountain. Can you come and get me, sis, quickly, please? I am dying to give you a hug."

MUDI

15th arrondissement

The last room of the Modigliani exhibition was dedicated to a Virtual Reality experience.

The Museum meticulously recreated Modigliani's room and workshop near Montparnasse. The visit was organized on a "First come, first served" basis, and I joined the large queue of Modigliani's fans.

The brochure that a cheerful Museum employee gave me at the entrance informed that the room had been recreated to the finest detail, and probably it was exactly how the artist's studio looked like. I just had to put the VR headset on and enjoy the amazing journey.

The headset brought me into a small room, ochre in colour. I saw a small untidy bed with a few sardine tins underneath, a table with a full ashtray on it and a few chairs. The window was open and was letting some dim light in. There were a few paintings hanging on walls and one was resting on an easel, half finished.

I read the instructions. All was easy. I had to touch

the dot in front of my eyes, and the VR would tell me more about this place in Modigliani's room.

I touched the dot above the bed. A text popped up:
Although he continued to paint, Modigliani's health deteriorated rapidly, and his alcohol-induced blackouts became more frequent...

I suddenly noticed a blurry figure in the background; it slowly approached the table, and sat down. Then it became more visible: it was a tall robust man in a brown velvet jacket. He was poorly shaved; big drops of sweat were scattered on his beautiful forehead. He took a cigarette from his pocket and lit it.

I poked the man, expecting a text to pop up.

"Ow!" I heard.

I poked again, right on his nose.

"Ow!"

Much louder.

I couldn't have misheard the second time.

"Strange" I thought. "What's the interest of that?"

I touched the image again. Now it was his leg.

"Hey, you! What the hell is going on?" I heard.

I coughed and looked around.

"Yes, you! Sitting there and coughing. Who are you and why are you poking me?"

I took off the VR headset. A guy with "help" pinned on his shirt hurried up to me.

"What's wrong?" He asked with a robotic smile.

"Is it an interactive VR?"

"What do you mean?"

"Is it supposed to ask us questions?"

The guy pursed his lips together.

"Who is asking you questions, Madam?"

"Nobody, sorry, sir... I am just being stupid." I smiled apologetically and put my headset back on, hoping that the strange guy had disappeared for the sake of my sanity.

But he was there, finishing his cigarette.

"Oh you are back! " he said. "Where are you going to poke me this time?"

"What's your name?" I asked quietly.

"What do you think my name is?" He shrugged, pointing at one of the paintings. "What is yours, mysterious creature?"

"Anna" I said. "Anya, rather."

"Russian?" he smiled.

"How do you know?"

"Anya is Russian. I was madly in love with a Russian Anya once," he sighed, putting his cigarette out. "You can call me Dedo."

Somebody touched my shoulder. I took off the headset and saw the Help Guy.

"You've been talking, Madam."

"Is it forbidden?"

"You are not supposed to talk."

"Why?"

"You don't talk during the VR experience."

"OK."

"Just rules, Madam."

"OK."

"Please don't disturb others."

"OK."

"Hey," I whispered once back in the room. "They don't let me talk to you!"

"Where are you?" Dedo was comfortably lying on the bed, smoking another cigarette.

"In the museum."

"Doing what?"

"Visiting a Modigliani exhibition."

"Like, a whole exhibition?" he sat up on the bed.

"Of course, it's a big deal, like, the exhibition of the year. All the newspapers are talking about it. They brought paintings and sculptures from museums all over the world and also from private collections."

"Private collections?"

"Yes. You know, those paintings are worth millions."

"Millions of what?"

"Millions of anything."

"And who are those people who collect them?"

And then, before I could say anything, I swear to God, the ceiling opened and something fell on the Ochre room floor!

I looked closer: it was a man, a Chinese man in his late 50s. He was sitting in the middle of the room, terrified, looking around in astonishment, and it was obvious that like me he was new to this unusual VR experience. Not Dedo though. He calmly observed the man, and said:

"Nice suit."

"Thanks," the man nodded, checking his tie and making sure his glasses were placed impeccably on his nose.

"Great tie, too." Dedo approved, blowing smoke rings. One. Two. Three. Four.

"Dolce & Gabbana," confirmed the Chinese man.

"Italian?"

"Yes."

"Where are you from?"

"I am from China."

"And what are you doing so far from home, Chinese man?"

"I am travelling around Europe buying art for my collection... But hold on!"

He finally stood up.

"What is this place? One minute I am having lunch with the museum director, and then all of a sudden I find myself here. What is this place?"

"It is Modigliani's workshop. A VR experience." I intervened. "But I have no idea how you got inside."

"Modigliani? Mudi?"

"Modigliani," I repeated.

"Mudi," he nodded. "You know, I bought one of Mudi's paintings the other day."

"Really? Which one?" Dedo raised his head from the sardine tin he was carefully opening.

"Some naked woman."

"Was it expensive?"

"Oh yes. It was the second most expensive painting in the history of art. I saw it on the front page of a catalogue."

"Do you like the painting, Chinese man?"

"It is a good investment and I like the story behind it. But I must admit that if he hadn't thrown himself out of the window at the age of 35, the painting wouldn't be worth millions today. I probably wouldn't have bought it."

"He threw himself out of the window?" Dedo took a sardine from the tin and bent his head back. Then he sent it down his throat.

"It was Jeanne who threw herself out of the window!" I said and I poked the Chinese guy. "Modigliani died of tuberculosis!"

"Jeanne threw herself out of the window?" Dedo looked at me.

"You didn't know?"

"I guessed she would do that. I just didn't know for sure."

"Who is Jeanne?" The Chinese guy frowned.

"Do you like the painting?" Dedo swallowed the sardine.

"It's a naked woman with a long neck."

"How much money did you pay for it?"

"One hundred and seventy million."

"One hundred and seventy million for a naked woman with a long neck?"

"I paid for the story behind it. It is tragic and romantic. People like it."

"I see." Dedo nodded, thoughtful.

"How can I get out of here?" The Chinese guy begged. "I have to go home, to my wife, to my Art collection, to my beautiful investments. Please."

"Why don't you throw yourself out of the window?" Dedo suggested.

Somebody was shaking my shoulder. I hadn't noticed that the Help Guy was trying to catch my attention. I took the headset off.

"Madam," he said. "I have warned you. This is a noise-free zone. You are not supposed to talk. You are supposed to follow the instructions on the screen. Next time I will ask you to leave the VR room."

I looked at my fellow VR fans. They were slowly moving their heads in different directions. They sometimes slightly moved their hands and fingers or tapped their feet. It looked a bit creepy.

"Could you please just put your headset back on without disturbing the others?"

"OK."

"Thank you, Madam."

Dedo was standing by the window now, alone in the room.

"Where's the Chinese guy?" I mouthed.

"Threw himself out of the window, just as I suggested."

"I don't believe you."

"You don't have to."

"Did he really pay millions of dollars for the painting?" Dedo asked after some silence.

I nodded.

"For a woman with a long neck?" he smiled.

I smiled too.

"The front pages of a catalogue?" His curls were dancing joyfully. Dedo was laughing.

I laughed, too.

"And you know what?" Dedo pointed under the bed. "He stole my sardine tins."

He was right. They'd disappeared.

"A good businessman. They are probably worth millions!" I whispered, feeling that the Help Guy was approaching to kick me out of the room.

"Tragic and romantic figure!" Dedo exclaimed.

"Top dollar for sadness!" I couldn't resist laughter anymore.

Dedo was rolling on the floor in a fit of giggles.

"One hundred and seventy million dollars for a long neck!"

"For the last Bohemian himself!" I shrieked, and then... was immediately taken out of the room. The Museum walls were still shaking with Dedo's guffaws.

LIBERTÉ, EGALITÉ, FRATERNITÉ
11th arrondissement

I woke up in the strangest place.

It was a long tunnel with a pit in the middle. I looked down the pit: two long iron sticks were placed in parallel there with no beginning or end. Across the pit there was a long corridor with a few strangely dressed people standing in it. I looked around and saw some stones with an inscription:

"Vestiges de la Bastille".

With a closer look they did resemble the stones of the fortress. I was the right person to tell as I had spent quite a few years in this bloody prison. But what was this tunnel for and where did it lead? Before I could make any plausible guesses, a strange machine entered the pit: it was formed of quite a few white and green carriages and moved with incredible speed and noise. It suddenly stopped and opened its doors, like by magic! A few people came out of the carriages. They looked weird too: women in *pantalon*, men in thick *châles* around their necks, none of them wearing wigs.

One girl had quite an interesting *derrière*, only covered by a small piece of cloth; this incredible fashion was not from my times! I nostalgically saw the girl's buttocks off and went back to the reflection about my unusual situation.

When and where was I exactly?

I looked around again and O, Luck! A neatly folded *Gazette* was lying on the ground. I quickly picked it up and looked at the date. It was December the 2nd, 2019, exactly two hundred and five years since my death. The fact that I appeared in this strange tunnel on the anniversary of my death was rather puzzling. Full of questions, I thought it was time to look for a way out of the tunnel. It didn't take me long to find the sign "exit". Things seemed to be easy in 2019, I thought at first, but then I saw another sign: exits 2 and 3. Then: exit 5. 6, 7... all in all, I counted 8 exits. Which one to choose? I picked the Boulevard Beaumarchais one, as an honour to his wonderful theatre, and wondered if they had named any streets or boulevards after me. So, I followed the sign.

It was quite a labyrinth with stairs, tunnels and more stairs. The materials used for the labyrinth were different from my times; however, the smell was very similar. I noticed a few small puddles of urine here and there and a rat hiding in a dark corner. Bastille, like in the good old days! I climbed the last stairs and was finally in the street. Yes, it was *Place de la Bastille*. Everything was totally different from my times apart from one thing: it was full of people, shouting and screaming! I remembered July the 2nd, 1789 when I shouted into a funnel in the Tower of Liberty and urged people to tear down Bastille, this monument of horrors. The guards immediately considered me dangerous and transferred me to Charenton, but a couple of weeks later people did follow my advice!

But who do they want to behead this time?

I looked at thousands of people slowly moving in front of me, carrying big sheets of paper mostly calling for justice for all people. It seemed that two centuries later they hated the rich and powerful with the same fervour.

Was it another revolution?

To hell with the past, I thought, as the future was lying in front of me, opening its possibilities like a whore. The first shock was gone, and I was ready for new adventures, new debauchery. No better time for this than a Revolution!

I was slowly moving along the crowd, but still cautious about entering it.

Until I saw Her.

She walked passed me screaming something about Equality.

How cute, how innocent, how sensual!

"Égalité!" I could distinguish her soft voice in the crowd.

"É-ga-li-té!"

She was one of those girls you see once and you never forget. Being dead gave me courage, so I dived into the crowd, squeezing through it, in pursuit of this young flesh of extraordinary beauty. O, she was young! Maybe a little older than the sweetest age of sixteen, but she hadn't reached her twenties yet. The crowd was moving faster, so I had to be quick, too. My passion pushed me with inhuman speed, and soon I was able to see her again... She was petite and slim, delicate in her build. Her curly blond hair was covering her shoulders and I could already smell perfume on it. I moved faster, like a wolf chasing a lamb, and now was walking alongside her. Her profile showed a straight nose, a little narrow at the top. She probably felt my breath near her, turned her head, and smiled. She had the biggest and brightest blue eyes, showing tenderness and determination at the same time. I felt aroused and for a few minutes surrendered to my wildest dreams... Even though she was wearing a coat, I could still recognize her round and firm breasts underneath, I imagined them like two ripe apples... I tasted her pink smooth nipples, her silk belly... and went further down, even though that was not what I was after, to be honest...

The crowd had stopped for some reason; I took a few steps back and looked at the girl's *back gate,* incapable of breathing with excitement. Hundreds of whips were about to land on her round bottom and leave red marks on those hills of Eden... which, parted a little, would show her rosebud and promise me such tightness, such...

"Hey, *Monsieur*, could you move, please?" somebody pushed my back. Lost in my fantasies, I didn't see that the crowd had started to move again. I hurried to catch up with the girl.

She turned her head again and smiled. Her lips were bright red and juicy. I started to imagine how...

"What's your name?" she said suddenly and gave me her hand.

"I am Marie."

I decided to impress her with my aristocratic background.

"Marquis de Sade." I bowed.

"Very funny," she said. "But, seriously."

"I really like to be called Marquis." I decided to be honest with her from the very beginning.

"Are you into BDSM or something?"

"I am afraid I don't understand you, Marie."

"Oh, come on!" she gave me the loveliest smile. "There is nothing to be ashamed of. And, in any case, real sadists are there, surrounding us."

She made a vague gesture towards men in black, some with transparent helmets and shields. They were standing by the side of the road.

"Sadists?"

"The Police."

That's how they called the police in 2019!

Sadists. Was my name somehow involved in it or was it just a coincidence? In any case, I decided to add this new word to my vocabulary immediately to sound more modern and impress Marie even more.

At this moment the crowd moved forward, like a wave, and then was thrown back with incredible force. I tried to jump up to see what was happening, but made an awkward movement and nearly fell down. The crowd pushed me aside. I still didn't lose hope of catching up with Marie (now she was further ahead of me), making my way through the crowd, but every second it became more and more chaotic. All of a sudden, my eyes became watery and it was difficult to breathe; the air was hazy, and I heard somebody scream:

"These arseholes are using tear gas!"

I had no idea what it was and it bloody hurt, but I was obsessed with Marie and her *petit cul*, so I ran forward screaming "Égalité" to impress her. I also threw my wig into the crowd.

The next minute a long black arm grabbed my shoulder. It was one of the sadists.

"*Monsieur*, please follow me."

He was very tall, with absolutely square shoulders. I admired this symmetry for a few moments, and then he pulled me out of the crowd like a kitten. He took me to the side of the road, where another sadist was waiting.

"Your identity."

I decided not to reveal my true aristocratic background to the sadists, and humbly said:

"Citizen Donatien Alphonse François Sade."

"Stop this circus," The Second Sadist pushed me slightly. "Your identity card."

"You wouldn't believe me..."

"No, we wouldn't. We will continue this conversation at the station."

I had been successful escaping the forces of order a few times during my life, including prisons, so I thought I'd give it a try.

"Dear God!" I screamed, pointing at the opposite direction. "What the hell..."

Those imbeciles turned their heads exactly where my finger was pointing, and that gave me time to escape. I ran as fast as I could; I was chasing the girl. I had to get back to her now that we started a conversation, the mere thought of her tight buttocks made me shiver... And then I thought what if she introduced me to some girlfriends of hers... I could imagine them all so well naked, receiving punishment one after another...

"Citizen Sade!"

I tried to get deeper into the crowd, but The First Sadist took me by the collar, and dragged me from the crowd again, like a little puppy.

Now he stood in front of me, holding me tightly with his left hand, while taking something from behind his back.

Then, he deftly pulled both my wrists together and clicked some kind of shackles on them. Clink. Clink.

"You shouldn't have shown resistance to the law." He said calmly. "You will be taken handcuffed to the station."

"Handcuffed?"

I looked at the metal rings holding my hands together. What a difference to the heavy awkward shackles we had during my time! Amazed, I was looking at its sophisticated, yet simple mechanism. They were light and of adjustable size. Put on in a few seconds, a simple key would open them when needed. A work of genius! The victim would have to beg for the key...

Meanwhile they put me inside a carriage and closed the door. In 2019 the carriages moved without horses.

"Where are we going?" I asked nonchalantly." Is it going to be the dirty Picpus prison or maybe Charenton madhouse?"

I had spent 32 years in different prisons and madhouses during my lifetime, so I knew most of them pretty well.

"I guess the madhouse eventually all things considered," The First Sadist sneered. "But first to the station for your identification."

"Is it far?"

"Around the corner. Why don't you just stop asking questions and shut up, you are a real pain in the ass!"

That was the irony of my fate: I was going to add another prison to my long list. But as long as I could write and have my white nougat and peaches in eau-de-vie...

I looked at the shackles again. Where was I in my considerations? That's right. The victim pleading on her knees: give me the key; I'd do anything for the key. Anything, anything, anything! I imagined Marie and her girlfriends all handcuffed in one of the rooms in my La Coste Castle, and the cruelty of the key in my hand burned my skin...

"This is us!" The First Sadist announced.

He turned his huge body to get out of the carriage, and then I saw what I call perfection: a black stick was hanging from his belt, elastic, whippy, with a handle looking like a work of art... How come I hadn't noticed it before?

"What is this tool?" I asked in awe, pointing to the stick.

"This?" The Second Sadist frowned. "Are you joking?"

"No! Please, please tell me what it's called!" I begged.

"It's a truncheon. Would you like to taste it, too?"

I wouldn't. But I knew somebody who would. O, in so many different ways and places! I couldn't wait to get to my prison cell and give my fantasies all the freedom I could. I just hoped the sadists would give me paper and feathers or whatever they write with these days.

And peaches in eau-de-vie, of course.

LION, GIRAFFE, CHAMELEON AND BABOON
12th arrondissement

*(Written by The Ghost of Jean De La Fontaine
At Parc Zoologique de Vincennes, April 2019)*

The Lion, King of all the beasts
Of land and water, South and East,
Was pacing, angry, in his place,
Forgotten his Majestic Grace.
"O, fate!" The Royal Beast exclaimed,
Of my position I'm ashamed,
Humans don't like me anymore,
They have decided I am a bore,
They hardly come to see my cage,
And call me relic of Old Age.
This situation is deranged,
The times have absolutely changed!

"They have indeed!" – Giraffe replied.
Look at the matter from my side:
On longest neck my head is placed
And big horizons can embrace,
Yet, no one is keen to know
The unique vision I can show,
My boring days I spend in peace
Being a vegan I chew leaves,
The more organic is the better,
Though it doesn't really matter.

"Let us agree to disagree,"
Chameleon squeaked from a tree
You need some protein, my friend
Insects are healthy to this end.

Your eyes see far, I shall agree
To see the big picture is the key,
My eyes rotate up, down, in, out,
No small detail can be missed out,
And please consider my deft tongue,
So entertaining for the young,
Like magic, I can change my skin,
Of many colours I have been,
I know how to please their eyes,
I am the Master of Disguise!
In spite of these fantastic gifts,
I feel like falling from high cliffs.
My popularity is lost,

I still don't understand the cause.

"You poor lot!" - sneered Baboon.
Those humans love ME to the moon.
My messy hair makes them laugh
They cannot get of it enough
Their crowd will get bigger soon,
I'm happy to be their buffoon!
I entertain them with my lies
But only joy lives in their eyes,
I throw stones, I dance, I fart,
I talk of trees as if of art,
Bullying the weak, I praise the strong,
This tactic never proved me wrong!
A hundred tricks high up my sleeve,
While I perform, they'll never leave,
It's their sad and shocking fate,
They worship clowns, not the Great.

THE MUMMY
1st arrondissement

Anna and I are drinking rosé at mine and I am telling her this incredible story.

Something crazy happened to me, I say, and I light a cigarette. You have to listen to this. I finished work early the other day and decided to go to the Louvre.

Anna looks surprised.

I needed to take a break, a breath of fresh air, do something different after work, which would not be working or drinking, I explain. The best way to escape from reality is to go to a museum.

Anna raises her eyebrows and refills our glasses.

Anyway, here I am, in the Louvre Museum, I continue. It was not too busy as it was near closing time, and November is mercifully free of tourists. To cut a long story short, I got in fast and decided to go to the Egyptian room. I'd visited it ages ago, when I was a teen. I'd been impressed by huge cats and colourful sarcophagi and

The Mummy, of course. Have you been there?

Anna nods and mumbles: years ago. Then she swallows an olive, takes another sip of rosé and impatiently sighs. So?

So, I say, I decided to start directly with The Mummy. I found my way to the room and got closer to the glass cubicle where it was supposed to be. But I only found an empty sarcophagus there. I looked at the inscription: The Mummy. I looked down at the empty coffin. Looked at the inscription again. Where the hell was The Mummy? I looked around, but I was alone in the room. I thought maybe they put The Mummy into a different sarcophagus or removed it from the Louvre altogether, but there were no signs or explanations anywhere. I was about to go and ask a sleepy museum guard about what was going on when I heard quiet laughter. It was a different kind of laughter, not the one of a tourist or a museum employee. It was like something coming from *beyond*. Maybe I remember it like this now and I was just attracted by some unusual noise back then. I cannot tell. In any case, I turned my head and saw some strange movement in the sarcophagi room, which was situated just behind the Mummy room. I went there. High glass walls protected colourful sarcophagi and all of them seemed quite similar to me. Apart from one, in a quiet corner, almost hidden from eyes and mobile phone cameras. That's where the laughter was coming from and that's where I discovered something incredible...

Can I take one of yours, Stephanie? Anna says, pointing at my cigarette packet. You shouldn't ask, I say, and I refill our glasses. Now, Anna, listen to this.

I saw The Mummy sitting on the edge of a sarcophagus. Holding a roll-up in his hand, he was playing with smoke rings. Don't ask me how he let out the smoke; his head was totally covered with some greyish bandage leaving no holes for mouth or eyes. But he did. He did let the smoke rings out of his mouth and then said: Hey.

Anna looks at me with suspicion. I don't blame her.

I don't blame you, I say. It does sound strange.

Anna observes me for a few seconds and refills our glasses.

What about the smoke alarm? She says and slurps her rosé. How come it didn't go off?

How the hell would I know? I say. Maybe he disconnected it. Maybe it was a special Mummy smoke that couldn't be detected.

Ok, Anna shrugs.

Does she care at all about what I am telling her? Does she think I lost my mind? I can't tell.

Anna, I swear to god, The Mummy wanted to chat! He asked me my name and what I was doing there. I told him that I had just finished work and wanted to do something different from working or drinking that evening. I told him I was a French teacher for adults. I told him that some people learned French with me for business or pleasure.

And what did he say? Anna asks casually as if we were gossiping about a next-door neighbour.

He was surprised that some people study French for pleasure, I say.

Anna laughs. Did you speak French with him, Stephanie?

Actually, yes, I nod. His French is good. He only made some minor mistakes. He mixed up a few tenses and he didn't always use the subjunctive correctly.

You are such a bore, Anna says and refills our glasses. But please, continue.

Then he told me about his work, I say. He said that it was always emotionally draining when you work with people. Actually, he was having a cheeky cigarette break. Otherwise he had to lie down there all day. He complained that his work was hard. Imagine, some visitors read every inscription, take photos from every possible angle, stay staring at him for ages, never mind groups of teens who are particularly exhausting. Then he said that it was nothing in comparison with what Mona and Venus had to endure.

Like, Mona Lisa? Anna scoffs.

That's what I figured, I nod and open the second bottle.

This is good wine, Anna approves. Did The Mummy mention anyone else? Anna impatiently scratches the bottle label.

He didn't have time. We heard some steps

approaching. The Mummy hurriedly extinguished his cigarette and ran to his sarcophagus. I begged him to wait and answer what it all meant. How come he was... alive?

And what did he say? Anna's eyes are glittering in the dim kitchen light. She *does* care, after all.

The Mummy looked at me, then looked down at the empty sarcophagus, then at me again.

You know what, Stephanie, to hell with it! He said. I am sick and tired of lying here, and I need to take a break, a breath of fresh air, do something different...Then The Mummy winked at me and laughed, Anna. He had this deep laugh. It was quite a pleasant laugh, actually.

I am taking you on a trip to a different Paris, my dear, the one hidden from most, the one full of ghosts and different dimensions, he said.

He grabbed my hand and before I knew it we were at the back door. Somehow it led directly to *La Place de La Concorde*.

And what did you see there? Anna frowns.

First, I heard a voice, I say.

Anna grabs the bottle to refill our glasses, but puts it back on the table after some hesitation. A voice? I hear her concerned whisper. Whose voice?

Marie-Antoinette's voice, I say firmly.

And this is where the story begins, my dearest friend.

THE CURSE
2nd arrondissement

1.

The minute the guillotine chopped off my head, the crowd on *Place de la Revolution* cheerfully welcomed my death:

"Long live the Republic!"

Sanson, my executioner, picked up my bleeding head and lifted it on high. They wanted my blood. They needed it. They had it now.

To my surprise, the crowd didn't stay much longer after the execution to savour my blood and my defeat. I soon heard a few people say:

"It is already quarter past twelve; it is lunchtime, we must get home quickly."

"What time is it? I am starving!"

"Shouldn't we hurry for lunch?"

Lunch! That is all they could think about.

People were leaving *Place de la Revolution*. So was I.

The executioner threw my body into a cart and was about to place my head between my legs, when the skies opened and an angel picked it up saving me for eternity. What a relief! At least, this is what I thought. I was so naïve back then!

The Angel took me high in the sky, and we started to float like birds, leaving the cruel city of Paris underneath.

I looked down and saw my reflection in the Seine. All my suffering made me look like an old woman. My hair was completely white. It was also ridiculously short, since they had cut it before the execution. Hélas, it had nothing to do with the high pyramids of beautiful curls I had once been known for.

I was the Queen of France, put on the Throne by God Himself, and I was expecting a hearty welcome from him. Oh, do not get me wrong; I had sinned! But I had always been a righteous Catholic, I prayed and I confessed, and I was expecting at least Purgatory or even Paradise. I was also hoping to see my three little darlings that he had called so early!

I tried to ask my Angel a few questions, but he was ignoring me completely. He looked like a cloud, dressed up in a uniform with blue, white and red stripes, and had a very arrogant expression on his face.

"Are we going to meet God directly?" I tried again

after a while, but in vain.

As we were flying, the Earth faded away little by little; we passed over the clouds to some new layer, light and chilly. I saw a Palace in the distance.

The doors of the Palace opened when we arrived, and the Angel took me to a dark room with a pillow on the floor. There was nothing else there.

The small window gave a view of Nothingness. I was clearly not in Paradise.

"Where am I?" I asked the Angel.

"You are here temporarily. You'll wait for your judgment here."

"But I have just waited for my judgment on Earth for years, and look where it has taken me!"

I wanted to point at my severed head, but I forgot that I didn't have fingers, so I just made a choking sound instead. Considered that there was not much left of my neck, it was quite an undertaking!

However, the Angel's expression didn't change.

"It's revolution time, as you should know. God is very busy."

"Look," I said. "There must be a misunderstanding here. Do you realise who I am? I am the Queen. I must have priority. God chose me. I shouldn't be waiting here like an ordinary mortal, don't you think?"

"No, I don't," and the Angel locked the room from outside.

The room sank into darkness.

"This must be Hell, then." I thought. "At the same time, it is a little too chilly for Hell. In any case, I should be judged first".

I decided that I'd sleep on it. I was sure that it was nothing but a misunderstanding.

I woke up the next morning, and a dim light coming into the room gave me some hope. "They'll come to pick me up soon." I decided, but it was not before a few weeks or even months that I heard the door unlock. I lost track of time. You see, the time perception is different when you are stuck somewhere in eternity. Yet, the same grumpy Angel appeared on the doorstep and announced:

"He is ready to see you."

2.

God didn't look like I'd imagined him: a big man with a beautiful beard, dressed in white, with big hands and a firm, but kind look. God in front of me had nothing to do with what I'd expected. He was wearing a white dress indeed, but it looked shabby and I noticed a stain of something greasy on his belly. A funny hat with a cockerel embroidered on it covered his bald head; he had intelligent, but indifferent blue eyes.

"Marie Antoinette of Lorraine and Austria, widow of Louis Capet, the Queen of France." I bowed my head as low as I could. I was getting used to my new existence without a body, but some situations were still quite awkward.

"I know who you are." God said. His breath smelled of cheese.

I started to feel worried about my Austrian head.

"I dare to hope the Lord Almighty shall be merciful and allow my soul to enter Paradise eventually," I bowed my head again.

"It doesn't work like this anymore," God sounded impatient. "Times have changed. We have developed a more sophisticated and fair system of judgment."

"I didn't have the opportunity to confess all my sins." I said. "But I addressed them all in my prayers to you. I hoped you would grant me your mercy."

"I don't have time to listen to that. I mean, the prayers. There are too many people and too many cases. And all the priests' reports are a complete waste of time. I have my agents to put together a file, and then they bring it to me. "

I heard my sweat dropping on the floor directly from my head. I was probably in Hell, after all.

"No, you are not in Hell." God reassured me. "I would never give them such a diamond!"

I realized that he had thoroughly read my file.

"And as I have said before. The ideas of Heaven and Hell have much changed over the past years. Let's call it all one big Purgatory."

He was getting excited. He fidgeted around, and a big pile of paper appeared in front of him.

"Shall we start, *ma chère*?"

He took stylishly framed glasses out of his pocket, put them on and started to read:

"You were beheaded for high treason and also for incest with your son. These are serious sins, to say the least."

"Wait a second...this is Earth judgment. First of all, as God Almighty you must know that it didn't happen that way, and I should be judged here for different matters, too."

Goodness, I must have sounded so rude. I just kept making mistakes!

I bowed showing him my submission.

"It is written in your file. Do you doubt my sources? Because if you do, it means you doubt your God, dearest Marie-Antoinette."

"I would never dare to, my Lord!"

"I went through your file a couple of times. It is like reading an adventure book. Very entertaining. And very immoral."

"That's a history book, not a book of my soul." I protested.

"Ok, let's have a look at your soul." And he went through a few pages. "Madame Deficit... Versailles... The diamond necklace... I had so much fun reading this bit!" he lifted his index finger.

"You know, I get all kinds of *genres* here. Many files are just boring short stories. Or novels. Those are the worst: the longer they are, the quicker I fall asleep reading them. I get some poetry from time to time, thank goodness. There is a great deal of social drama recently, too. Well, you wouldn't understand that, you are too far from anything social, aren't you? Oh, here it is! Your soul in all its beauty, *ma chère*. Here we go: *Let them eat cake!*"

"Pardon me?"

"*Let them eat cake!*" God repeated with satisfaction.

"I am afraid, I don't follow, My Lord."

"On top of everything, you are a liar."

"I really don't understand."

"Well, it reads here: *Upon being alerted that the people were suffering due to widespread bread shortages, the Queen replied, "Then let them eat cake."*"

I couldn't say a word.

"You are the Queen who once said 'Let them eat cake'. The one who doesn't care about the poor, whose cynicism has no limits."

"I've never said that. This is something people must have invented. A rumour. A misinterpretation."

"You mean, millions of people are wrong? How pretentious of you!"

"May I suggest the Lord Almighty verify this?"

God rolled his eyes.

"You really should go to Hell!"

The door opened and let the grumpy Angel in. He

hurriedly came up to God and whispered something into his ear. He looked preoccupied.

God nodded thoughtfully. Then he said to me:

"We are living in difficult times, *ma chère*. I have so much work that I really don't have any more time for explanation or verification. You should forgive me for this. But you will see and understand everything by yourself, don't you worry."

Then he clapped his hands and everything went black.

3.

I call him The Big Man. He can't see me, just like anybody else, but I grew really fond of him, and I speak to him in my mind sometimes. As if I had a friend. I am sure we would have become really good friends under different circumstances. Over the past two hundred and something years, I have seen many people come and go here, but The Big Man is still my favourite.

He starts early, preparing thoroughly for a long working day.

I love watching him! Luckily, I (my head) settle comfortably in my corner and observe him with a smile.

Soon, the customers start to come in. This place is

very famous, and it attracts many tourists as well as locals. Rightly so: these intricate, magnificent walls are full of grace and history. A real Master who at the time worked for Louis XV founded it in 1730! If I were visiting Paris, I would definitely come here every morning too, for History and for Pleasure.

The Big Man is always very polite and friendly, and has great style. He is in his fifties now, but he looks wonderful in spite of his remarkable belly. How can you not be a bit on the plump side working in a place like this though? I sometimes think that he feels uncomfortable under my observant eye even if he doesn't see me. Or does he?

I then rotate to see the outside of my habitat. It is fascinating too. Montorgeuil Street is one of the loveliest and liveliest streets in Paris; there is a café opposite and also a butcher's. I would give anything to be able to sit outside, on a terrace and watch lazy Parisians pass by. I have seen so many changes, victories and troubles, but they sit and they sip their coffees and wines, year after year, decade after decade, watching life. Hélas! Like I've said, I can only rotate, but I cannot leave my modest corner next to some salty delicacies and cooked meats; it is right in front of the main counter.

It gets really busy during the day. From the long and impeccably decorated counter people buy brioche and macaroons, éclairs and baba au Rhum; they order cakes of different types: white and dark chocolate, strawberry, raspberry, pistachio and apricot, with and without cream; they pick huge meringues piled up on the counter near the bottles of fine champagne and jars of fresh juices.

Then the night falls, and the Big Man closes the front door.

I am finally on my own and I can think about God. I send him as many prayers as possible, even though he did warn me that he didn't have time for them. But I am an optimistic person and I hope that one day he will re-examine my file.

Meanwhile, I spend eternity watching people "Eat cake".

THE TRUMPET
8th arrondissement

Monsieur Le President of Cinema Gaumont,

I am writing today to give you a detailed description of the incident that happened at Cinema Gaumont Champs Elysees, on June 23 of the current year. The mystery of this outstanding event hasn't been left unnoticed by my colleagues and unfortunately has caused a few complaints from our audience.

As a head projectionist and the main witness of the case, I consider it my duty to inform the senior management about my version of events.

That evening it was business as usual. It was my second projection; we had already opened the movie theatre to the public even though the film wouldn't start for another half an hour. I was bored, so I observed the audience for a while. I have always found it amazing to watch people, especially in the cinema.

I remember that day a few elderly couples slowly

took their seats first, and then the movie theatre started to fill up little by little. There were a few students in scruffy jeans, a few couples who started cooing and giggling as soon as they took their seats, and some "loners", as I call them: those men and women who come to the cinema on their own, quietly sit down and wait for the film with some air of sophistication. I noticed a very tall guy with a cloud of blond hair. He looked like a giant dandelion! I recall wondering who would be so "lucky" to sit behind him. He chose a good seat. Well, it was his right to have the best angle for the screen. It is not his fault that he is so tall, after all.

In the middle of a food delivery ad, where four teenage girls are dancing, overwhelmed by a giant pizza, there was a bright flash of light, and the ad disappeared, leaving the screen blank. A split second later a man started to appear on the screen. At first there was his trumpet and his hand. The body followed the hand and the head slowly grew on the body. I had seen this man before, and it only took me a few minutes to recognize him. The interesting thing was that the audience didn't seem surprised, but rather annoyed. They started looking around, shrugging, and whispering. I quickly realised that they were probably NOT seeing the guy on the screen! None of them, except for one. The Dandelion guy! His jaw literally dropped and then he exclaimed: "Boris Vian?"

I must admit I was happy he said it, because as you can imagine, I was in a state of shock, too. As a *projectionist, I knew perfectly well what was on each reel; and Boris Vian had never been there.*

We also realised (we: me and Dandelion) that Boris was "live".

He looked a bit surprised at first, but then smiled and performed quite a decent trumpet solo. Then he bowed:

"Good evening!"

Things went even crazier after that. A spotlight appeared from nowhere and lit Dandelion's hair; when I say, "lit" I mean it figuratively, of course.

So, Dandelion was in the spotlight. Once again, the audience could not see it.

"Hello, Dandelion." Boris said.

Dandelion blushed, but said firmly:

"Hello, Boris. What are you doing here?"

He is a brave guy, this Dandelion, I thought, observing the scene.

"I am here to watch a film. Last time it was interrupted because Death swallowed me like a Giant Sole Fish!"

Few people remember it, but Boris Vian died when he was watching an adaptation of his book "I Shall Spit On Your Graves". Ten minutes after the projection had started he said that he didn't believe what he was seeing and then he had a heart attack.

And now he was back and he wanted to see a film! I was wondering what he was going to think about it.

It was an adaptation of a book, too.

We adapt more and more books to films, I think. On

the other hand, I must admit, some adaptations are not bad. The book authors are mostly pleased with the result, so is the audience. Photography and special effects have become extraordinary, but we lack some good narrative, something new. We just keep recycling: adaptations, biopics, autobiographies, remakes of the classics, fairy tales...

But back to the point!

"Welcome!" Dandelion showed Boris the empty seat next to him. "I would be honored if you joined me."

To be honest, I was a little worried about the situation, because I wouldn't know what to do if Boris had a heart attack again. Should I call the ambulance in this case? It wouldn't make sense, unless they could resurrect him from the dead. At the same time, it is our civil and moral duty to call an ambulance if somebody is having a heart attack, no matter dead or alive...

While I was lost in those thoughts, Boris disappeared from the screen and jumped onto the seat next to Dandelion.

Thank goodness, the ads came back immediately, and I hurried to start the film.

The public seemed reassured.

I was observing the audience, preparing for the worst.

A few minutes later somebody sneezed.

It is weird how many people actually get a cold during the summer, I thought. I've heard people sneezing even on the hottest summer day.

Another couple of louder sneezes followed.

Again.

Ahchoo.

Ahchoo.

Ahchoo-Ahchoo-Ahchoo.

There was a pattern there, I thought, a rhythm.

No normal human being would be able to sneeze like that.

It was Boris Vian.

The worst thing of all was that this time not only Dandelion could hear it, but everybody in the audience.

After the tenth sneeze, I heard a humble but firm cough. You know, those expressive coughs when you are "hinting" that you are disturbed in a public place.

Then more coughs followed.

Cough-cough.

Ahchoo.

Ahchoo.

Ahchoo-Ahchoo-Ahchoo.

Cough-Cough-Cough.

Ahchoo.

Cough.

Ahchoo.

Cough- Cough- Cough.

Then finally a woman stood up and squeaked in desperation:

"Could you please stop sneezing?"

"Yes, we cannot hear the movie properly!" a Baritone agreed from another part of the movie theatre.

But there was no way he'd stop.

He just kept sneezing.

Why was he doing it?

Was it the new air conditioner that we had installed in the cinema two weeks before?

I find it very powerful and not very good for the environment, to be honest. I caught a cold the next day after its installation. Boris Vian could be reacting to this cold monster, too.

Another explanation would be an allergy.

Who knows?

Dust on the seat, popcorn or Dandelion's perfume.

We are all human, after all, even when we are dead.

Maybe he was allergic to the film, quite metaphorically?

At the same time I was relieved that he didn't die 10 minutes after the movie started, like he did last time, but does it mean that we adapt books to films better nowadays?

I am still wondering if he was enjoying the movie we were projecting that day.

All that sneezing...

As you know, it was so disturbing that most people left the cinema without finishing the film, and we received a few letters of complaint.

I should have stopped the projection, but if you think about it stopping the projection because somebody has an urge to sneeze would be wrong, wouldn't it?

When the film finished and a few people who had stayed hurried to the exit, I saw Dandelion standing up from his seat and saying:

"Bless you, Boris!"

A funny guy, this Dandelion, isn't he?

Then he slowly walked to the exit.

Boris started to disappear the opposite way from how he'd appeared: his head first, then the body, and then the hand. His trumpet was still lying on the cinema seat, though.

"Boris, you have forgotten your trumpet!" I shouted. Now I was alone in the cinema.

No answer.

I went down to Boris' seat and picked up the trumpet.

It looked so lonely among empty popcorn boxes and coke cans scattered all over the place.

I took the trumpet home and I take care of it now.

And this is how my story ends, Monsieur Le President.

Yours truly,

Julien Muller,
Head Projectionist.

LOVE HEIST
9th arrondissement

"What a horrible winter we've been having this year!" Sonia tightened her checked Kashmir scarf. "The coldest in decades, I bet."

She was going up Rue Jean Baptist Pigalle, cringing from the merciless glacial wind and endless January drizzle.

"This city is unbearable in winter," she thought. "Brutal and bloody cold."

"And ugly." She was approaching Place Pigalle.

"Tourists visit Place Pigalle as some tribute to a decadent and bohemian *époque*, but look at the reality! What can we see here now? A supermarket. An overpriced organic shop. A tacky nightclub. Homeless people with homeless dogs scattered everywhere. This is a new trend, humans have more compassion for animals than for other humans, and give more money to humans with animals." Sonia concluded.

"Anyway," she sighed. "Here we go." She pulled the

bank door. "Let's go get some cash".

The bank was quiet at that time of day. On the left, near the entrance there were a few ATMs; a middle-aged man in a grey jacket and a gloomy hat was withdrawing some cash, another man in a similar outfit was queuing.

A bit further on the right a bold guy in a navy blue jacket was yawning at the reception desk. He looked indifferently at Sonia when she came in, yawned again, and went back to his computer screen.

"All Parisians look the same in winter. Grey, navy blue and gloomy." Sonia took her purple gloves off and joined the queue. "What a drag!" she opened her leather bag and pulled out a small mirror and a lipstick.

"This winter is killing me," she examined her pale face. "Or is it just that after forty little can be done? Isabel was talking the other day about injecting vitamins under the skin. She says they have nothing to do with Botox, and all that crap. But I was wondering if ..."

Her thoughts were interrupted by noise coming from the front door. It slid open, and two men appeared in the bank.

One ran straight to Sonia and hid behind her, and the other took out a gun and shot in the air. Once. Twice.

"Oh, my God!" Sonia dropped the lipstick.

To Sonia's amazement, nobody else in the bank reacted. The receptionist was falling asleep in front of his computer. The ATM guy in a gloomy hat was waiting for his money.

She decided to do like they do in films: lie down on

the floor, even though nobody gave her instructions to do so.

"It's better to anticipate," she thought, putting her hands behind her head.

"What are you waiting for?" she whispered to the young man who was hiding behind her. Now that she was lying on the floor, he was standing there, all by himself. "Lie down unless you want to get yourself shot!"

"This is so much fun!" He lied down next to her.

"You are out of your depth, boy!" Sonia mouthed. "This is not "fun". This man has a gun."

He is so young, Sonia thought, having a closer look at her fellow hostage. Seventeen? Eighteen maximum. And God! Doesn't he stink? He must be one of those homeless people who camp at canal Saint Martin or even here, Place Pigalle. Where is this country going? Now not even young people have a decent home. What is he even doing in a bank? He must have come here to warm up, as simple as that. It is freezing outside. And his clothes, for Christ sake!

Reflecting on the difficult fate of homeless people in Paris, Sonia didn't notice Gun Guy approach. When she looked up, he was right in front of her.

"Get up!" He roared.

Sonia followed the instructions. After all, she had three small children.

"You could have been a bit more polite." She mumbled. "People have lost the minimum respect for others across all industries nowadays."

"Not you!" Gun Guy shouted. "Him!" He aimed his gun at the homeless boy.

"It's not him who has the money! Shame on you!" Sonia couldn't hold her anger anymore. "It is not poor kids like him who rob this society, it is the bloody banks! So leave us people alone!"

"Madam," she heard the reception guy. "Could you please stop disturbing others? Please speak quietly if you really have to speak in a bank. Otherwise you could just go outside to speak on your phone or whatever you are doing there, don't you think?"

Then he went back to his screen, but he didn't acknowledge Gun Guy at all. As for other clients, the first ATM bloke had left, and the second was examining his nails, waiting for his cash.

This is not a bank robbery, Sonia thought.

"This is not a bank robbery at all," she said quietly to the boy. "He is after you," Sonia continued, pointing at Gun Guy.

"I know!" the kid said. Then he reached the back of his head, found something there and threw it into Gun Guy's face. Then he did it again.

"Why didn't you tell me from the very beginning?"

"I was going to, Madam, but this bank robbery game of yours was so much fun!" He threw another *something* into Gun Guy.

Sonia looked closer: he was throwing lice into Gun Guy. Big, fat, gross lice that were swarming in his hair.

The most disgusting thing she'd ever seen.

"And you don't like him either," she commented on the third louse flying towards Gun Guy.

"I hate him!"

"How dare you, Rimbe!" Gun Guy stamped his foot. "You, little bastard, you ruined my life. And I am finally going to finish you off!"

"You ruined it all by yourself, love." Rimbe said calmly.

"Rimbe?" Sonia frowned.

"Arthur. My name is Arthur. But he keeps calling me Rimbe, like before. Centuries have passed but he still calls me Rimbe and he still cannot leave me alone. He's been chasing me through eternity to kill me. He failed once, you know. It was a long time ago, in Brussels. This keeps him awake at night. He wants to "finish me off". His name is Paul, by the way."

Paul scratched his beard. He was not an example of cleanness and taste either. He stank of alcohol and there were big yellowish stains on his old-fashioned black jacket. It was probably vomit.

He looked around and put his gun in his right pocket. Then he took a flask from the left and opened it.

"What is this lousy place anyway?" He asked. "Where is the bar? What happened to *Le Rat Mort?*"

He took a sip and put the flask back into his pocket. Then he took out the gun again.

"*Le Rat Mort?* What is *Le Rat Mort?*" Sonia asked Arthur.

"On this very spot there used to be a "bohemian" bar called *Le Rat Mort* but in reality most of the people who came here were just Parisian bourgeoisie who thought they were poets and intellectuals."

"*Les Bobos,* I know the type," Sonia nodded.

"Fucking bastards." Arthur continued. "I was bored to death. Paul here loved their company though. He loved sharing his poems, too. I commemorated my presence by a painting produced with my own excrements, right over there," he vaguely waved his dirty index finger. "Made a great impression. Not as big as my poems, of course. Revolutionary stuff, you know." He added with satisfaction.

"So, you guys are poets?"

"Haven't you heard of *The Arsehole sonnet?* We wrote it together among other things."

"Not as I remember..."

"Well, to cut a long story short, I am a genius, and Paul is not too bad."

Paul blushed, but didn't say anything.

"But why *Le Rat Mort?* Why this name?"

"I think somebody found a dead rat while fucking here one day, but maybe it is just a legend."

"It is still full of rats, anyway." Sonia shrugged.

"It's a bank, right?" she clarified and then looked at Paul:

"Could you put away your gun, Paul, so that we could talk like civilized people?"

Paul ignored her remark, and did the same ritual as a

few minutes before: put the gun into his pocket, took the flask out, took a sip, put the flask back, and took the gun out.

"I see you are a troubled couple," Sonia continued. "Have you tried counselling?"

"What the hell are you talking about?"

"You need a third person to help you."

"Like, a threesome? Hey, Paul, this sounds more fun than your boring accusations and your recent interest in the Catholic Faith." Arthur giggled.

"He is not a Catholic, is he?" Sonia looked at Paul with reproach.

"He is. He has become one after prison."

"I knew he looked like a criminal!"

"He is. He shot me in the arm. Twice."

"Stop provoking me!" Paul clenched his teeth.

Then he carefully opened his coat and put his hand inside, searching for something in his inside pocket.

Rimbe sneered.

"And what are you up to now, pocket man?"

"This!" Paul pulled out a penknife, carefully wrapped in a murky cloth.

Now as Paul needed three objects at the same time: the flask, the gun and the penknife, he was showing amazing juggling skills keeping all three within reach.

"I recognize this penknife!" Arthur said. "Remember what happened the last time we did it here?"

"Did what?" Sonia asked, turning pale.

"You know, Paul and I used to play this game. It

started here, in this place. I mean, there." He showed to the stairs leading to the second floor. "At the bar. We were drinking with other so-called poets. They were reading their so-called poems. One day I asked them all to spread their hands out on the table. They did it thinking it was a joke. Paul did it too, of course. I told them it was an experiment, ha! I pulled out this very knife from my pocket and slashed Paul's wrists. By the way, dear, how come you have this penknife now? Anyway. I then stabbed him twice when he tried to run away, in the thigh. It was quite exciting. We did it a couple of times later. Stabbing each other in public places. So pro-vo-ca-tive, they used to say."

Then he carefully approached Paul and stroked his cheek.

"Hey Paul, why don't we go and check out the upstairs. Instead of killing me we can do some fun things together, like in the good old days, don't you think?"

"Paul, I loved you. I really did. I still do." He added in a whisper.

"You won't find anything exciting up there; only some bankers offices," Sonia said.

"We can have fun one more time, can't we, Paul?" Arthur was looking his miserable lover in the eye. "Madam's bank robbery idea really appeals to me, and we have all we need. Or we can just kill them all. Or stab them. Nothing personal, you know. Or political, as Madam here would have liked. Just pro-vo-ca-tive. Just a game."

Paul made a sipping noise and gave Sonia the flask:

"And then I'll kill him." He pointed to Arthur.

"No, thanks, Paul, very kind of you." Sonia gently refused the flask.

Paul threw away the flask and cocked his gun.

"Get out of here, Madam! It's going to be hot, boiling hot in here!"

"Will you be ok, guys?"

"We have all we need."

"Good luck then."

"We don't need it, Madam"

"We are already dead!" Paul lifted his gun in his right hand and slapped Arthur's tight buttocks with his left.

"Have fun then, guys."

"Maybe you'd like an autograph before you go?" Arthur suggested.

"Another time," Sonia smiled and headed to the exit.

"I am going mad." She inhaled the humid January air, carefully closing the bank door behind. "What the hell was that? They make me think of..."

The gunfire interrupted her thoughts.

It was coming from the bank.

Once. Twice.

"I hope they've killed the banker," Sonia gave a coin to a homeless man sitting near the bank entrance.

"Thank you so much, Madam." He bowed his head.

"What are their names?" Sonia pointed at the dogs next to him.

"Rimbaud and Verlaine. I know it sounds a bit strange, but they used to come to the place called..."

"Le Rat Mort. I know. I know." Sonia came closer and stroked one of the dogs.

"And Paris has just become warmer, don't you think?" she added, smiling.

TO THE GREAT MEN, THE GRATEFUL HOMELAND
5th arrondissement

Pierre, I want you, and only you to share this story with; as my companion, love of my life, but also because you have always been fascinated with the spirit world.

I became a spirit for a day, and went back to Paris on July the 4th 2019. Just imagine, my Pierre.

The first discovery was that both you and I are buried in The Pantheon. The fact that we rest together in this honourable Mausoleum filled me with joy and pride. I spent some time there among sleepy tourists and finally found my way out to the beautiful July Paris.

Where would you go? What would you do? I can only use my imagination, dear Pierre.

You'd be surprised to know that I didn't want to go to The Sorbonne or any other university, or any laboratory. You see, I dedicated my life to Science and just wanted to spend some time on my own, feeling alive again. Who would have thought? Also, you know the scientific community: they would have never believed in some resurrected Nobel Prize woman scientist wandering the Earth a century later, even if it were only for a day.

I did watch students near Sainte Genevieve library though, and that moved me a great deal. After all, they haven't changed that much; they have different haircuts, but their youth and strength are tangible even from a distance.

I felt hungry.

Do you remember how in my early Parisian years I survived on bread and butter because I was so poor? Then, once we got married I "cheated" with stews and soups just to make plenty of food for a few days and free up as much time as possible for my studies? Remember how bad that cooking was? I know you do, my love.

I couldn't use my outstanding culinary skills this time for obvious reasons, so I decided to have a bite at a local restaurant; you know I don't like to waste too much time eating, but at the same time it is a great way to listen to people and understand what's going on.

I was curious, so I went into the first restaurant that met my eye.

A friendly waiter gave me the menu; I chose the cheapest dish (it sounded Italian) and a carafe of water. He politely took my order and then said:

"Are you from Romania?"

I found it funny as my language has completely different roots to Romanian, but I politely answered:

"No, as a matter of fact, I was born in Poland."

"Yes, exactly!" He looked satisfied. "Somewhere from Eastern Europe! I have good ear for accents, don't you think?"

And he happily hopped away to give the order to the kitchen.

Meanwhile another customer arrived, and she was seated at the table next to me. Pierre, you know how it used to be in Paris in our times, the cafes and restaurants with so little privacy. In 2019 it is even worse: people literally touch their neighbour's sleeves and hear them chewing their food.

The lady next to me was elderly, seventy-five or even eighty maybe, but she looked well and was confident on her own.

She sat down and ordered a set menu with a carafe of water, too, but her water was never served. She kept asking the waiter who was hopping by, but he was too busy with other customers.

I finally turned to her and said:

"Would you like some water?"

And I poured her some of my carafe.

"Thank you," she nodded.

"You are welcome." I smiled and went back to my fatty pasta, but then heard her say:

"You are not French, are you?"

"I am."

She raised her eyebrows.

"I am." I repeated.

I was full of self-assurance and somehow it convinced her.

"Oh, I am sorry, Madame, it is not what I meant. I meant you have a foreign accent. I was just wondering where you came from?"

You know how stubborn I can get when somebody annoys me.

"I am French."

"Not Romanian? You sound like somebody from Eastern Europe!"

Was she plotting with the hopping waiter?

But that was just the beginning, Pierre.

Next, I was sitting on a bench (no more restaurants for me, thank you very much!) and observing the incredible city Paris had become. I was lost in my thoughts and amazement when somebody coughed right into my ear (you know how I feel about this, Pierre):

"Excuse me!"

There was a lady standing in front of me, probably my age.

"Are you a tourist or do you live here?" she asked.

That was an unusual way to approach somebody, don't you think?

It was a difficult one to answer, too.

On the one hand, yes, I was a Parisian. On the other hand, I hadn't lived there for nearly a century.

"I am visiting," was the most appropriate answer I could find.

Her eyes became two small peeps.

"Do you know where the Saint Michel metro is?"

"I am afraid I can't help you," I said quietly. Her eyes almost disappeared from her face in the attempt to understand me.

She sighed and then shouted:

"DO YOU KNOW WHERE THE SAINT MICHEL METRO IS?"

"I am afraid, I can't help you." I said calmly.

"SO YOU ARE NOT FROM HERE!"

"Please, don't shout." I asked. "I understand you perfectly well."

"THANK YOU!" She shouted, and left me on my bench half-deaf.

Not much has changed in Paris after all, Pierre.

I wandered around The Pantheon for a while thinking about what our grandchildren have become. I was also thinking about the research and the consequences of our discoveries. Maybe I should have visited the Lab, after all?

I was lost in my thoughts and didn't notice what was going on around me. You know the feeling, my love. I am sure you were far away exploring your genius ideas, when you had your atrocious accident.

Before I knew it, I bumped into a young woman and spilled some coffee she was carrying in a plastic cup.

(A strange way to have a hot drink, isn't it? Mind you, it saves so much time for more important things!).

But now the woman's dress had a huge brown stain on it.

I apologized.

"Oh please, do not worry!" she smiled.

I didn't really worry, to be honest, but I apologized again.

"Forget about it." She reassured me. "It is just a dress."

"I was lost in my thoughts," I said.

"I bet you were." She looked at me closely. "Would you have a coffee with me?"

Why on Earth would she offer that? However, my curiosity said: "With pleasure."

We were near the Sorbonne, so I thought I could have a coffee and then go to see the University. I thought maybe she worked there. Maybe she could tell me things about this new future world.

"Let's sit outside," she brought two coffees. "My name is Bénédicte. Béné."

She had beautiful blue eyes and was probably in her late thirties. I liked that she didn't sit too close to me, keeping a comfortable distance between us. She inspired trust, you see.

I told her who I was. She wouldn't believe it anyway, I thought, but at least I wouldn't have to lie and pretend to be somebody else.

"Of course, I believe you, *Marie*!" Béné sipped her coffee. "And I have so many questions for you."

She did indeed. She asked me about our times, about our lives and our research; I told her about the day you had your accident, and her eyes filled with tears. I told her about the war, about my losses and struggles, I told her about Paris back then, and she told me about the 21st Century. She told me about our children and grandchildren who continued the research. Listen to this, Pierre: she took a flat rectangular machine out of her bag, and found out everything about our grandchildren in a few minutes. There is an encyclopaedia that you can access from anywhere any time without going anywhere, although Béné did say that it was not always accurate. Our grandchildren were alive! I was thinking whether it would be possible to find them in the few hours I had left as a ghost and whether it would be a good idea.

Meanwhile, Béné took a packet of cigarettes out of her bag and lit one, thoughtful.

"So, how long did you live in France?" she asked.

"44 years."

"44 years?"

"Most of my life."

She let out smoke and looked at me, smiling. She had that smile, Pierre, and that special French way to purse the lips.

"The most amazing thing of all," she shook her head, "is that after all these years living here... And then being dead, for nearly a century, but also here, in France, I don't know if this counts... Nevertheless... You've never lost your Polish accent!"

And then she took my hand and said:

"It is quite strong and you *still* have to work on it, don't you think, Marie?"

UNCLE VITYA
6th arrondissement

"Are you ready to order?"

"We'll have eighteen oysters, number three, please, the small ones." I pointed at the menu. "No, better twenty-four. Two dozen?"

"Dvye duzhiny?" I translated for my parents and their best friend Vitya who don't speak French. Jojo, my French boyfriend smiled politely.

"Da, nas zhe pyat." My mother nodded.

"Yes, since there are five of us." I agreed.

"Somebody will have one oyster less." Jojo protested.

The waiter cleared his throat.

"Yes. Sorry," I continued. "A bottle of champagne, to go with the oysters. Two dozen oysters, right? Actually, two bottles of champagne, please. And then, five "menus philosophe" because we are in such a place..."

I double-checked the choice with my guests.

"What language are you speaking?" The waiter asked.

"Russian. They've come from Russia to visit us." I

pointed at my parents and Vitya.

"That's what I thought," he said with a hint of a smile and left.

"This is an amazing place, my dear child. Thank you." Vitya put his delicate hand on my shoulder. In fact, I have always called him Uncle. Uncle Vitya.

He was already drunk, but it didn't show much. He easily combined heavy drinking with his job as a doctor but drank double when he was on holiday and triple when he was on holiday in France. He was sixty-five years old, but he'd never thought of retirement. He was always well dressed, perfectly shaved and wore expensive perfume. Not too much though. Everything about him was tasteful and measured, except the insistence with which he proposed toasts.

As soon as the champagne and oysters were served he solemnly stood up and said:

"My dearest, beloved friends. I'd like to raise my glass to this surprising place. The thought that I am having this champagne at the famous Procope, founded in 1686, the place where Voltaire had his coffee, Robespierre, Danton and Marat had their meetings, and Napoleon once left his hat... it makes me proud."

I summarized this briefly for Jojo who spoke very little Russian, sipped some champagne and poured shallot sauce on my oyster. Then I said:

"Uncle Vitya, these oysters are excellent, don't you

think?"

He smiled.

"I agree, my dear child, exactly like my mother loved them. Small and with a dash of shallot sauce on top."

"Let's drink to Vitya's parents!" My mum stood up. "Unfortunately they passed away a couple of years ago, but they lived a long and happy life".

Jojo tried to reach everybody's glass to "Chin-Chin!" the toast but he was immediately told off because Russians do not clink glasses if the person they drink to is dead.

"We also drink in complete silence in this case." I added.

Uncle Vitya's mobile phone chimed.

"Speaking. Of course not, Ivan Sergueevich, of course you are not bothering!" He made big apologetic eyes and mouthed "sorry" to the rest of us. "You are more than welcome. It's our job. Yes, your mum's results are perfect. She will live to be 100. Ha-ha... The best care, as always. No doubt. Wonderful, have an excellent evening, too..."

He hung up and sighed. "I never stop working, even on holidays! Even in Paris, for God's sake. But this patient of mine, or her son, to be precise... He keeps bringing me potatoes and tomatoes to express his gratitude. Potatoes and tomatoes, my dearest friends! I can afford to buy them myself, you know." He laughed. "Yet, there is something touching about him, something authentic," he adjusted his glasses and stood up.

"My dearest, beloved friends! I would like to raise this glass to our people! French, Russian, it doesn't matter. To our workers. They are clever, honest and strong. My grandmother had newspapers for curtains in her room after the Second World War. The poverty was extreme, but she never gave up. Please let me raise this glass to all peoples and my grandmother!"

"Can we clink glasses now?" Jojo whispered.

"No, she is still dead, don't you get it?"

We drank without clinking our glasses again as the tradition demanded.

At that moment I noticed a strange movement around the empty table next to us. It looked like a grey shadow of a man with long curly hair, old-fashioned style, a middle-aged man wearing a wig, like a judge. I closed my eyes for a moment and slightly shook my head. But when I opened my eyes the man was still there.

"Dementia tremens? Hallucinations?" I wondered, observing the man who was quite transparent, but with a rather visible silhouette. He was drinking coffee and smiling sarcastically.

I was brought back to reality by my father's voice.

"Well," my father cleared his throat. "Let's drink to Svetlana, Vitya's sister. She was a wonderful woman."

"Now, what shall we do?" Jojo pinched my leg.

"Nothing. Just drink in silence. This is to Uncle

Vitya's sister. She died last year from liver cirrhosis."

I noticed Uncle Vitya staring at me.

"I am saying that your sister died, Uncle. Just translating."

Uncle Vitya scoffed.

"This is so relative! She is not really dead."

"Well..."

"Death doesn't exist, my child." Uncle Vitya insisted, smiling.

"Well, theoretically..."

"It just doesn't."

He stood up. He had got to the point when he barely sat down. He was wobbling a bit, too. He clinked two glasses to draw everybody's attention. Clink. Cliiink.

"Tolstoy said: How rich our Lord is! My dearest, beloved friends, look around. Look at these walls, centuries old; these art objects, these sublime paintings on the walls. It is our eternal beauty, eternal happiness. We all will leave this world very soon, but you shouldn't worry because death doesn't exist. My dearest, beloved friends, death doesn't exist, don't you get it? I've come to understand this recently. Don't be afraid of anything, my beloved. Because one day - and this day is closer than you think - we will see everything and everybody. Not here, but *over there*," he pointed to the ceiling. "We will see Leo Tolstoy. We will see Fyodor Dostoyevsky. We will meet Robespierre and Marat, Diderot, and Voltaire..."

At that very moment I heard an unpleasant high-pitched voice going:

"Nonsense!"

It came from the table on the left. Our transparent neighbour had a voice. I even knew who it was. I swear to God, it was François-Marie Arouet, commonly known as Voltaire. He looked just like in his pictures; only the bags under his eyes were much deeper. Also, his wig had slipped to the left and looked dirty.

"What nonsense, Death doesn't exist! How wrong you are, Doctor!" Voltaire shook his head.

"Incredible," I thought. It was obvious that Voltaire was talking to Uncle Vitya, but Uncle Vitya didn't speak French. He couldn't understand Voltaire even though he definitely heard, maybe even saw him, judging by the expression on his face.

Did Voltaire want me to interpret for Uncle Vitya? No way! I was fed up with interpreting for Jojo so I pretended not to hear anything.

Meanwhile, Voltaire continued.

"I am completely dead and my death was long, atrocious and painful. Like your wife's, Doctor."

Uncle Vitya sadly looked at me. Voltaire was right; Uncle's wife died 10 years ago of some nasty uterus cancer and her death was indeed atrocious. Cancer destroyed, swallowed, turned her into dust within 6 months; not even money, the best hospitals or the most advanced technologies could make her live longer. I remember sending her a box of her favourite chocolates and white wine, and she kept it until her last day hoping that I'd be there to share them with her. Uncle Vitya and his wife didn't have children of their own and I was like a daughter to them. But I arrived too late and I couldn't say good-bye to her. Cancer was stronger and faster than anything else.

"Look at this beauty!" the waiter brought us the main course.
"This is gorgeous!"
"It smells so good!"
"A bottle of red, here..."
"White for me, with the fish..."
"Enjoy!" the waiter poured the wine.
We continued chewing and sipping.
"Would you like to try some of my *coq au vin*?"
"Yes, just a little."
"I am so full!"
"Some more wine?"
"Yes, please."
"I wonder how they cooked the vegetables. The texture is amazing."
"This meat is very tender, too."

I looked out the window. It was getting dark and it was getting late.
Voltaire was still there, seemed bored and even more transparent. He was finishing his third cup of coffee.

"This awful coffee won't keep me awake, don't you worry!" Voltaire reassured me, noticing my interest in his caffeine intake.

My parents started yawning. Uncle Vitya was now leaning over the table and had slight hiccups.

"My dearest, beloved friends. I raise this glass to our Lord, to our faith, to our bright, unique, essential faith. Do you remember Dostoevsky? Do you remember one of his characters saying, "If God does not exist, everything is permitted"? There is nothing without God and his will. No-thing! The Lord is everything. And he will give us the eternal life we deserve. He is kind and wise. He is our only hope. He watches our every step. To the Lord!"

"To the Lord!" I raised my glass making a sign to the waiter to bring me the bill. Quickly.

"God doesn't give a damn and doesn't care about your every step, Doctor." Voltaire scoffed.

Uncle Vitya looked at him sadly.

"He is just quoting himself, Uncle," I reassured the poor man.

"Please, stop annoying Uncle Vitya," I asked Voltaire. "Can't you see? He has nobody in the world. Absolutely nobody. Everyone dear to him is dead."

"This is not the reason to become a "Slave of Christ", as they put it."

"How enlightening!"

"Just humanistic. I've been drinking coffee here for

the last two and a half centuries, listening to people, observing them. Incredible things have happened, progress seems to take over even though I must admit that coffee has got so much worse. And yet people cling to their old gods. Nothing works for them. Whatever they can do to trick Death. But it is always Death who tricks them."

Voltaire finished his fourth coffee, and stood up.

"It was a pleasure!" He grinned and walked to the exit murmuring something to himself.

The waiter brought the bill.

"Please, wait!" I begged Voltaire. "Maybe you could stay a little longer? Maybe you could keep Uncle Vitya company?"

There was no reply.

"Who are you talking to?" my mom asked, putting on her jacket.

"Nobody."

My father helped Uncle Vitya get up.

"Let's go. We are the last clients. The restaurant is closing." He said.

"Nobody." I repeated quietly, looking around. I was hoping to see at least a glimpse of Voltaire.

But he was not there. As if he had never existed.

¡COJONES!
14th arrondissement

It was insomnia, once again.

Jean-Baptiste was tossing and turning in his small hospital bed, counting sheep, trying to convince himself that his mind and his body were exhausted, and sleep was the only solution to this never ending fatigue. He must be thinking of nothing, pure nothing, and then slip into unconsciousness.

In vain.

Jean-Baptiste opened his eyes. The dawn was starting to break, and the sky was of the amazing violet-blue colour only possible in early July. Jean-Baptiste sat up on his bed and wiped tiny sweat drops from his forehead. No point in trying to let some fresh air in: windows don't open in mental hospitals.

He looked around: another bed, empty. An ugly chair and a bedside table next to it. A wardrobe, with a broken handle. And then, of course, himself, pathetically sitting on his bed at four o'clock in the morning in a baggy Rolling Stones T-shirt: "Let's roll!"

It was one of the rare moments when Sainte-Anne hospital was quiet; most of the patients were asleep, and those who didn't sleep were under heavy sedation.

Jean-Baptiste was neither; he just sat up on his bed, contemplating the intense violet-blue outside.

"You have a visitor!" He heard a deep male voice.

Before Jean-Baptiste could say anything, the door opened, and a huge man walked in. He was almost two meters tall, with an immense chest and strong shoulders. He looked like a warrior, a hunter, a powerful giant. He was carrying an enormous paper bag.

Jean-Baptiste knew he was not hallucinating, even though such certainty could sound inappropriate in a mental hospital; the mysterious guest was really there: he slowly walked through the room and landed on the windowsill.

"Ernest," he said, opening the paper bag. "But many call me *Papa*."

He took a big plate of oysters and a few bottles of wine from the bag, and said:

"The place where I used to have oysters and wine near Contrescarpe is closed now, but they have some decent offers on oysters and wine in this neighbourhood, too."

"At four in the morning?"

"Why not?" Papa said, pushing the cork inside the bottle with his huge sausage-shaped thumb. "I guess you don't have any decent glasses here?" He sent half of the bottle down his throat. "Want a little sip too? An oyster?"

He had a funny way of pronouncing his L's, Jean-Baptiste thought. A slight lambdacism, one would say. Decent gwasses. A wittwe sip.

"Oysters make me sick, and I don't drink," Jean-Baptiste said, "and who the fuck are you, anyway?"

"I am a writer."

"Ernest Hemingway then, I hope?"

"Ernest Hemingway. Himself. You are a clever son of a bitch." His guest nodded. "But please, call me Papa."

"Are you a hallucination, Papa?"

"No, I am a ghost."

"This really helps! Makes a big difference in a mental hospital, don't you think?"

Jean-Baptiste got up, came closer to Papa, and started touching his wide face and white hair, like blind people do sometimes, but Papa immediately pushed him away:

"What are these *mariconadas*?"

"Wanted to double-check."

"Papa is telling you that it is real, it means it is real. Have a sip of this wine." He insisted.

"No, thanks. I don't drink anymore."

"That's why you are here?"

"No. I am here because of my book."

"Are you a writer or something?"

"I wrote a book."

"What about?"

"About war."

"What war?"

"The Algerian war."

"And it led you here?"

"Indeed!"

Jean-Baptiste opened a drawer and took out a book with a black and white soldier on the cover.

"*The Wound.*" Papa went through a few pages. "How do you know about the war?"

"My family story. Also, I was a war journalist, just like yourself."

"That was a long time ago. You have anything new to say about war?"

"I do. I wrote this autobiographical book as a part of my therapy for depression. The story starts back at the end of the 50s when my mother had a fiancé who was sent to the Algerian war. Three days before the end of his service he was killed. He had left a letter..."

"Hang on!" Papa frowned, finishing the third oyster. "You are not going to tell me the whole goddamn story?"

"Why not?" Jean-Baptiste scratched his cheek. As Papa's mouth was busy with the oyster, Jean-Baptiste hurriedly continued:

"He left a letter to his best friend making him promise to take care of my mother in case of his death. His best friend, who is – ta-dam! - my father- kept the promise. They got married, had three children: my two sisters and me. Many years later, when I was a teenager, my mother got depressed."

"The one who had a fiancé at the war?" Papa started

the second bottle.

"Yes, yes, just listen! You see, she decided that she hadn't mourned her fiancé long enough and did not have the right to be happy. You get it? Years later, her guilt, like a time bomb, invaded her and took her mind away! She ended up in a Psychiatric Unit, and your humble Jean-Baptiste here became fascinated with war and decided to become a war journalist. I wanted to die there just like my mother's fiancé did, see the connection? Fucked up, isn't it? I went there looking for my death, ha! I didn't die, though. In fact, war kept me alive. I did them all: Chechnya, Kosovo, Iraq. After a few years of being a war journalist, I developed a strong PTSD, and was not allowed to write about war anymore."

"PTS what?"

"I became depressed. It was a big deal. Opening my eyes in the morning took a huge effort. Eating something- a heroic act. Cleaning after myself- just impossible. I didn't give a shit about living in shit. Even two fat rats in my kitchen didn't bother me much. I ended up here, in this hospital. My psychiatrist advised me to write my mother's story, and then to move on. He said writing would help me a great deal. And it did."

"You were not even wounded at all those wars?"

"No, nothing ever happened to me."

"Pity. Only wounds can make you a real soldier, a real warrior. I went to Paris and then to Italy in 1918 and was severely wounded; I know what I am talking about. A bomb exploded a few meters away; the Italian next to me was instantly dead. I had two hundred and thirty-seven wounds in my leg. They managed to save it somehow. I was terrified. But this incident didn't scare me off Death, of its danger. On the contrary, I felt invincible. From that moment on, all my life, and especially my writing, was fuelled by it. You cannot write anything worth it unless you've hurt like hell."

"I've hurt like hell seeing my mother unconscious in her own vomit and excrements. That was because of a war, its consequence. It was only a different type of wound."

"Of course, as the fat bitch Stein would put it "You are a lost generation". It was not even her who said it first; it was a *garagiste* guy here in Paris. He complained about people not being able to do things properly after the war. You are all a lost generation, he said. Stein just repeated it, but I turned this sentence into a classic. So, you don't have to tell me about *those* wounds. I wrote books about them myself."

Jean-Baptiste took a packet of cigarettes out of his pocket, opened it, looked inside, took out the lighter, clicked it a few times, and put it back into the cigarette pack.

"Hey, Papa, do you think you could try and open the window a bit? With some effort, we could make a little one or two centimetres gap. I am dying for a smoke. I don't have much strength in my arms, but you are a real giant, huh? I could then smoke, standing on the windowsill."

Papa pushed the window. It squeaked and let a centimetres of fresh air in.

"Thanks," Jean-Baptiste jumped onto the windowsill. He then lit his cigarette and blew smoke out the window. Papa looked at him.

"What I don't quite understand is why you are here again "because of your book". You said it was a therapy, which is nonsense; no literature is ever a therapy."

Jean-Baptiste nervously dragged on the cigarette.

"When the book was finished, I thought: maybe I could publish it. Maybe I could turn this pain into Art, something beautiful, you see. My friend found me an agent and before long the book was out there. And listen to this, Papa: it was a hit! All major French newspapers and magazines were talking about my book; all the literary blogs recommended it.

"Simply the best book about war in recent years." People loved it! Some Algerians wrote to me, with gratitude. I travelled around France and told people the story over and over again. I appeared on TV. I won two prestigious prizes.

"Critics and prizes are all chickenshit, I didn't even go to pick up mine. All phonies." Papa shrugged, and finished the second bottle.

"Of course, I hadn't expected such a success." Jean-Baptiste continued. "I was overwhelmed with my prizes. It was all new to me. I was so full of energy that I hardly needed any sleep. Three hours were now more than enough. I felt ten years younger. I felt omnipotent, too. I could do anything. It was easy. Everything was easy.

I was intelligent and charming: I was irresistible. I had countless women and zero regrets: I was insatiable.

I then went on a spending spree. I bought a new car as if it were a pair of jeans. I treated everybody to champagne in my local café. I gave 50-euro notes to homeless in my street.

And of course, I had at least ten new writing projects in my head. I could express any thought, and talked for hours, I just never shut up...”

“You still never shut up!”

“Then, my friend Pierre said one day: “Hey, J-B, something is going on here. Something is wrong in your head. Check it with your doctor. Just check. Just do it for me”. I laughed at him, of course, but went to see my psychiatrist, just to prove my friend wrong.

“See, doctor,” I said proudly. “I couldn’t be healthier.”

The doctor looked at me, silent. He observed me for a few seconds, then sighed: ‘You are having a maniac episode, Jean-Baptiste!’

Jean-Baptiste rubbed his hands together, with an odd satisfaction.

Papa burst out laughing:

“You went crazy again?”

“Yes, I was too happy this time. My brain just can’t get it right.”

“*I couldn’t be healthier, doctor!*” Papa wiped a tear from his cheek. “You are a real nutcase, *amigo!*”

"I lost it after my depression too, though." He added, still laughing. "I was paranoid about losing all my money, suspicious of my friends, I also thought I was followed by the FBI!" he raised his chin.

"FBI? What, seriously?"

"Yes, I was convinced that even some doctors in the hospital were FBI agents. That's why those sons of bitches administered electro-shocks! Ten, fifteen, more and more. When I was discharged from the clinic I was a vegetable. I was asked to write a few words in tribute to President Kennedy, and it took me a week of huge effort to write four simple sentences. Four goddamn sentences! I couldn't write, couldn't read anymore. It totally destroyed my memory. I was just chickenshit."

"That's why you put a bullet in your head?"

"Among other things. I was done: I couldn't see properly, couldn't have sex, couldn't drink and couldn't write. Wars, plane crashes, car accidents, my body and my mind were utterly destroyed. You know, everybody owes something to their Death. I owed mine some dignity, at least, after living so closely to her all my life...

What is there now for you, *amigo*? What is next? What do you owe and to whom?"

"Next? I have no idea. Have you ever known what is next?" Jean-Baptiste shrugged. "The sun is also rising over Paris. It is beautiful. Just watch it."

Papa pulled out a shotgun.

"Is this the one?" Jean-Baptiste turned pale.

"It is indeed. Paf!" he put it in his mouth.

"You don't have to do it again, do you?"

Papa shook his head and took the gun out of his mouth. "But it can still be of great use." He winked.

Then he cocked the gun.

"What the hell..." Jean-Baptiste closed his eyes, breathless.

Papa fired the gun.

The window swung open.

Papa was a great shooter.

"Much better!" Papa said with satisfaction, putting away the gun. "It is too stuffy in here, and honestly, watching such a beautiful sunrise over Paris through a dusty hospital window is a stupid joke, *cojones*! And you, *amigo*, deserve a proper smoke, don't you think? There is nothing worse that smoking through a ridiculous gap in the window, like a *maricon*, huh!"

THE EXQUISITE CORPSE[1]
17th arrondissement

"Could I have a cup of coffee, please?" Mrs. Martin waved at the bartender. The bar was so tiny that he didn't have to come up to the tables to take orders.

Mrs. Martin smiled and looked around: she was alone in the legendary Cyrano bar. It must get busier later, she thought, taking the Guidebook out of her bag and putting it on the table.

"Here is your coffee."

"Thank you," she immediately took a sip. "Excuse me..."

"Yes?"

"This book here," she shook the Guidebook, "it says that this bar was popular among the Surrealist Group at the beginning of the last century. They used to come here

---

[1] Exquisite corpse, also known as exquisite cadaver (from the original French term *cadavre exquis*), is a method by which a collection of words or images is collectively assembled. Each collaborator adds to a composition in sequence. This technique was invented by surrealists.

for an aperitif."

"So?"

"So, I was wondering if you know anything about it? Maybe an interesting story to tell me?"

"Which surrealist exactly are you after?" The bartender yawned.

What an odd question!

"Hmmm, Salvador Dali, for example."

"Anybody else?"

"I don't know." Mrs. Martin blushed. "Picasso? But was he a surrealist?"

"He had his days."

The bartender observed Mrs. Martin for a few seconds and concluded:

"Your French is not *too* awful for an American."

"Oh, it is not my merit." She laughed. "My grandfather was French."

"I see. Would you like anything else?"

"As I said," Mrs. Martin cleared her throat. "Is it true that surrealists used to come here for drinks and their famous games?"

"No," the bartender shrugged. "It is not."

"But it says here, - she quickly went through the Guidebook- 'The Surrealist Group used to gather in Le Cyrano.'

"You've been misinformed." The bartender walked back to the bar. "Actually, the Surrealist Group used to meet in a bar called Cyrano, but it was on *Place Blanche*. That "Cyrano" doesn't exist anymore. Your guidebook just mixed things up. The only Cyrano around is this one."

"There is nothing special about this place, then?"

"It depends on how you see things. In fact, you are not the only one who has been misled by the name *Cyrano*."

Mrs. Martin was about to ask more questions about other people being mistakenly taken to the wrong place by the untrustworthy Guidebook, but the bar door suddenly opened and let in a cloud of unbearable smell, followed by a group of decomposing creatures emitting horror-movie-like sounds.

Mrs. Martin nearly choked on her coffee and held her breath.

"Actors?" Her wishful thinking went. After all, the bar was next door to a nice little theatre.

"Zombies," reason answered.

The bar was full of zombies! The bartender, however, didn't seem to care much. He murmured "Bonjour", opened a newspaper and started to read.

Better stay quiet for now, Mrs. Martin thought.

The zombie crowd sat down at the big table near the entrance and she wouldn't be able to slip away unnoticed, anyway. The bartender's indifference gave her courage, too. He was not panicking, so why would she? Maybe they *were* actors, after all.

One of them looked almost like a normal human being. He was wearing a black suit and a bow tie; one could almost call him elegant if it were not for his dirty long nails and a gigantic disproportional head. His face, even though touched by decomposition, still held a resolute, nearly haughty expression.

He must be the Boss, Mrs. Martin decided.

The one who sat next to him drew her attention, too: there was something incredibly familiar about him. He had one of those hipster moustaches so popular nowadays among "cool kids" of Brooklyn.

Where could she have seen him? Mrs. Martin rubbed her temples.

Others didn't have many distinctive features or were too damaged by decomposition; apart from perhaps the short swarthy one, who was sitting by the door and giggling.

"Da-da!" he barked out, and immediately received a slap from the Boss.

"EX-PEL FROM THE CIR-CLE!" He yelled.

"Tra-la-la-la-la!" another zombie patted the Boss' back.

This one had the most charming smile despite the missing teeth; he was also wobbling and looked very drunk.

"The exquisite corpse!" The Boss uncurled his nail and raised his index finger.

All the zombies nodded enthusiastically.

"Let's begin, you, halfwits!" The Boss stood up.

"I will be the first today, Boss, to make the contribution to the *Creature,*" the short zombie took his right arm off and placed it on the table.

The Boss crossed his arms on his chest and solemnly

nodded.

"Next!"

The next one was the smiling drunk zombie. He contributed his left leg. Then he got all-emotional and wanted to contribute his right leg and his left arm too, but others disapproved, hissing and booing.

"One limb per person!" The Boss agreed. "Who wants to contribute his right leg to the *Creature*?"

"Me!" one of the zombies squeaked.

"Boss, this is not fair! He contributed two arms last week!"

"No, I did not! He is lying, Boss!"

"Stop it, colleagues. Can I at least stick my elbow on one of the *Creature*'s arms?"

"My arm will look beautiful on Him, too!"

"Look, Boss, isn't it gorgeous?"

"I will stick a couple of my nails onto his fingers, can I, Boss?"

"I'll contribute my leg anyway. He can have three legs, right, Boss? Or even four! Anything is possible in the surrealist world."

"Look! There is a place for another arm! Mine is small and half rotten. It will add extreme charm to the composition!"

"Enough! EX-PEL YOU ALL FROM THE CIRCLE!" the Boss shouted, but it took a few minutes before the bar became calm; the zombies were ecstatic, ripping off their limbs, exchanging elbows, decorating the new creature on the table with pieces of their hair, nails, ears ... One of them even found quite a decent piece of skin, which was rather a rarity in the zombie world.

"ORDER!" the Boss yelled again, took his gigantic head off and placed it on the octopus-like creature lying on the table. Then the Boss's arm reached out and tried to grab the Moustache from the Moustache.

"OUT-RAGEOUS!" the Moustache shouted, pushed away the hostile hand and presented his penis on the table.

"Small!" the zombies concluded, shaking their heads, but the Moustache crossed his arms on his chest, raised his head and closed his eyes. He totally believed in the importance of his contribution. He was adamant. So the penis was added to the creature, too.

Mrs. Martin felt the *Andouillette*[2] coming all the way up from her stomach and getting stuck in her throat.

Throwing *this thing* up could lead to a real catastrophe, given the circumstances. She has to keep it down.

Keep it down, keep it down, keep it down.

Why the hell did she have her grandfather's favourite dish for lunch?

Meanwhile, the zombies became so silent that one could hear a fly, or rather a dozen flies buzzing.

The octopus-like new creature moved, followed by an ecstatic "Oh!"

---

[2] Andouillette: A sausage made of pork intestines. It has a strong, distinctive odour related to its intestinal origins and components.

The look of it called for Mrs. Martin's *Andouillette* again, the bartender didn't even look up from his newspaper, but the zombies stared at the new creature in awe.

A few seconds later, the creature sat up on the table, stretched its various arms and legs, clicked its tongue and announced: *"The Exquisite Corpse shall drink the new wine."*

Those who had hands started applauding; others shouted "Bravo!" then a "Da-da!" followed, which was, in its turn, followed by a slap from the Boss.

The bartender was still reading the newspaper. He was absorbed in the Politics section.

"The Exquisite Corpse shall drink the new wine!"

The creature stood up on the table and stamped its foot.

"I heard you the first time!" the bartender rolled his eyes and put away the newspaper.

"Rosé, Blanc or Rouge?"

CHEMISTRY
19th arrondissement

A metallic voice announced, and the metro doors let in a tiny woman with a microphone.

Léa looked up from her book. The Tiny woman was standing right in front of her. God, wasn't she ugly! Look at her huge head swinging on frail shoulders, her wasted hands clinging to this dirty microphone. And the smell, man! She must have bathed in Chanel No 5 perfume. But she also must have eaten a ton of garlic. What a weirdo! She is not going to sing, is she? And who the hell is she winking at?

Léa looked around. There were very few people at this time of night, and nothing could disturb their Monday evening somnolence.

To hell with it, Léa stood up and changed her seat making sure that she sat with her back turned to Tiny

Woman. Offensive maybe, but there is nothing wrong with reading a book in peace.

BELLEVILLE.
BELLE-VILLE.

The metro doors clapped.
Right, where was she?
Here we go.
" ...a similar response occurred in our scanning study: those subjects who gazed at photos of better-looking partners showed more activity in the VTA. And the VTA is rich with dopamine..."
Heavy sounds of accordion interrupted her.
Where does this come from?
Tiny Woman was in front of her again.
What the hell?
She was singing. Her desperate rrrrs sounded like a drrrrill, but she was sincere. Authentic.
Like that girl Léa had met many years ago here, in Paris.
Her name was Chloé. She used to sing, too. Mostly in small Parisian bars. She believed that she only needed to keep falling in love to be happy, to feel alive.
Chloé had decided that she would always be in love, no matter what.
Léa had told her that she saw the world as a combination of pixels and was only interested in good sex. She added that she worked in advertising and she

didn't care. Chloé kissed her hand and looked her straight in the eye. And then she walked to the bar to get another drink. She had that way of moving her large hips, when walking.

All the pixels from Léa's old world fell apart in a second. Nothing was stronger than those hips swinging in a crowd.

GONCOURT.
GON-COURT.

But that was long time ago.

"Elevated levels of dopamine in the brain produce extremely focussed attention, as well as unwavering motivation and goal-directed behaviours. These are central characteristics of romantic love."

God bless dopamine.

All has a scientific explanation, after all.

There is some clarity for us, unfortunate subjects.

Fuck, not again. How come she constantly appears right in front of me?

Léa tiredly looked at the Tiny woman who was waving her hands and singing *La vie en Rose.*

REPUBLIQUE.
REPU-BLIQUE.

La vie en rose was Chloé's favourite cocktail at the

time, Léa smiled.

They used to come to that small jazz bar, and Chloé would go to the counter to order drinks swinging her incredible hips. She only drank two things: *La vie en rose* (champagne, vodka and peach liquor) or gin martini. Léa always had the same drink as Chloé. When Chloé was going for gin martini, she would always say "martinI". She dragged the final I as much as she could. It was diabolically sexy.

Tiny Woman was ecstatic. Tears were literally leaping from her big blue eyes, probably too big to be beautiful, but their expression made Léa shiver.

ARTS ET METIERS.
ARTS. ET. METIERS.

Enough homeless singer's emotional crap, though. What is wrong with her?

"Low levels of serotonin produce obsessive thinking- a central component of romantic love..."

They say bananas are good for serotonin, Léa remembered, scoffing.

Léa had read it somewhere when she was desperately trying to get Chloé back.

But Chloé was already in love with somebody else.

Their unique connection, the poems they wrote together bathing in the sunlight of hotel rooms, Chloé's wet morning hair: all was gone. She only loved Léa for a few months. It was nothing personal, just her chemistry worked that way.

And, to be absolutely honest, she had always preferred men.

RAMBUTEAU.
RAM-BUTEAU.

Tiny Woman was piercing the air with her Rs.

Tiny Woman was breathing in and out her sorrows with incredible clarity and honesty.

That was the only way to continue to live.

Léa closed her eyes.

HOTEL DE VILLE.
HOTEL. DE. VILLE.

God, Chloé, you were the most amazing creature in the Universe.

You were my light, my hope, my madness.

I hate you so much, Chloé.

Léa opened her eyes.

Tiny Woman was still standing in front of her, slightly out of breath.

She was fiddling with the microphone in her hands.

She looked beautiful now.

She should go easy on garlic, though, Léa thought.

CHATELET.

CHATE-LET.

Terminus.
All passengers, please leave the train.

"Your book!"
Somebody shouted.
"Hey, madam, you forgot your book!"
But Léa was already far, walking fast to the exit and leaving "Why we love: the nature and chemistry of romantic love" behind.

EPILOGUE
20th arrondissement

On the 3rd of July Camille went for her usual morning run at exactly 7am.

She usually ran near the famous Père Lachaise Cemetery, which was still closed for visitors and tourists at such an early hour. That morning, however, passing by the little side gate entrance to the cemetery from Rue de la Reunion, she noticed that it was open; after some hesitation she came closer and pushed it.

The little gate indifferently let her in; Camille climbed the stairs and once on Avenue Circulaire, she started to run. Père Lachaise looked more like a park than a cemetery, and that summer morning there was not a single cloud in the sky. Camille closed her eyes for a second, blissfully.

Amazing place, she whispered, passing Heloise and Abelard's grave. Hello, Mano Solo. So long, Bellini. A nice statue, Chopin.

"I heard people run here anyway, even when the

cemetery is officially open at 8am," she waved away a tiny sting of guilt. "I might not have another opportunity to have Père Lachaise just for myself..."

"Not just for myself though," she slowed down noticing two men drinking wine from small plastic bottles. They were comfortably sitting on a grave.

One of them looked familiar, but Camille couldn't remember where she might have seen him. It was difficult to tell his age; he wore dirty leather trousers and a grey shirt. He looked alive though, unlike his drinking companion who actually resembled a ghost and had a big dirty hole on his old fashioned jacket, right on the chest.

"I am not the only one disrespecting the dead," she chuckled. "These drunkards must have been partying here all night."

"Hey, young lady!" She heard Leather Trousers whistling mockingly. "Care to join us for a drink?"

Camille decided to pretend she hadn't heard, and kept running.

"Nice legs, don't you think, Fred?" Leather Trousers continued, but his friend didn't say anything. "Sure you don't want a drink with us, girl?"

"Pigs," she thought.

"Just one!" Insisted Leather Trousers. "Please."

"What the hell do you want?" Camille breathed in some courage and stopped. Although she stopped at some distance, she was not really afraid; in the worst case scenario she would just run away, and those unfit alcoholics would never be able to keep up with her young, healthy, 27–year-old legs.

"Just to talk. Really, girl." Leather Trousers said apologetically.

"Why don't you talk to your friend?"

"He doesn't have a heart."

"But he can still talk. People without hearts can talk."

"Not really. I see what you mean, but as a matter of fact he doesn't have a heart *at all*"

"What do you mean, he doesn't have a heart *at all*?"

"He sent his heart to Poland. Pickled in a jar of cognac."

"What nonsense!" Camille scoffed and turned away.

"No, please, don't leave. Speak to me a bit more. Please."

She came closer and looked at him. He used to be very handsome, she thought, and he still had very beautiful curly hair. There was something about him. Also, the cemetery was about to open to the public. She was curious.

"What's your name?" Leather Trousers asked, taking advantage of her momentary hesitation.

"Camille. And you?"

"Jim."

"Nice to meet you, Jim."

"And this here is Frédéric. Fred." Jim introduced his silent friend.

"The man without a heart?"

"Exactly. Sometimes I think that if I found some

cognac, this might bring him to life. I mean...err... not exactly to life, but to talk and to feel something, at least. He keeps me company sometimes, but he is not much of a conversationalist, as you can see."

Camille looked at the other man. If it weren't for Jim's friendly manner and reassuring July sun, she would have been scared to death. Fred was thin and very pale and nothing in particular could be read on his face. She looked at his fingers and saw that he was moving them slightly, as if he were playing the piano. His fingers were beautiful. He must be a pianist, Camille thought, or he used to be one. Unfortunately, the fingers were the only part that showed any life about that man. Everything else was immovable: his face, his eyes, his mouth. And he indeed had a hole instead of heart.

Jim put his hand through the hole on Fred's chest as if he'd read Camille's thoughts:

"At the last moment he asked to send his heart back to Poland, where he had been born. His sister smuggled it into Warsaw in a jar of cognac."

"So you think that if you two drink cognac, he might talk to you?"

"It could help, who knows? Like, some magic potion."

"Why do you drink wine then?"

"We drink what we can find here, girl."

"You mean you live here?"

"Yes, some strange destiny of mine. I am still trying to understand it. Why the fuck am I stuck in a cemetery forever."

"You cannot leave?"

"No," Jim sighed.

"At the beginning it was kind of fun." Jim continued. "The fans brought drugs and plenty of alcohol, mostly whiskey, my favourite. Now look at this place," he waved at the alley with a few graves. "A few withering flowers, a few cigarette ends."

"Now I have to search Modigliani's grave if I want to have a drink." He sadly complained. "People still bring him some booze. Not much though. These are difficult times."

"But I will gladly share it with you," and he gave Camille the plastic bottle with "Petit voyage. Merlot" on the label. "Sorry, we rarely find glasses here."

"I don't drink." Camille said.

"Come on. Just a sip. Be cool!"

"I don't drink alcohol. I mean, at all."

"No drinking in the morning type of girl?"

"In the evening either."

"AA?"

"No."

"Some serious disease?"

"No. I just don't drink alcohol. I don't do drugs. I don't smoke."

"Why?"

"I want to live a very long life. I care about my health."

"That's why you run in cemeteries?"

"Partly. Sport makes me happy, too. Endorphins, you know."

"Endorphins? Do you have some for me?"

"You can only produce them in your own brain."

"Cut the shit, girl."

"Maybe you could try to do some exercise or yoga."

"So, what you are saying is that exercise gets you high?"

"Yes."

"What a fucking load of nonsense... Say it again?"

"Say again... what?"

"That you are high on exercise."

"What for?"

"Just say it."

"I am high on exercise."

"Again," he mockingly pulled his right ear. "Again. Loud. I can't hear you!"

Camille rolled her eyes and prepared to wave her hand goodbye but Jim suddenly stood up and came closer to her. He took her face into his hands, pushed away her long curly hair, and then shouted "Boooooooo!" right into her face. " Booooo!" He repeated. "Booooo!"

Camille froze. "Ou-lou-lou-lou-louuuuu!" Jim tapped on his mouth like in some tribal ritual, and then took off his shirt, and started dancing around Camille, waving his arms and jumping on one leg, screaming "Booooo!" and making scary faces. She suddenly remembered where she had seen this man. Of course, why hadn't she realised it from the very beginning? Of course, it was him.

The performance didn't last long though; Jim was out of breath quickly and had to sit down, holding his hand over his heart.

"Bad heart too, you know," he complained.

"Nice performance," Camille said, clapping her hands.

"I am glad you liked it," Jim picked up a cigarette end from the ground and lit it. "Although what can you understand in such things if you've never been to the other side?"

"Like, doing drugs and stuff?"

"That's oversimplifying it, girl."

"Long and healthy life is worth it."

"Fucking hell, Camille. Are you serious? And what is "wanderlust" anyway?" He pointed at Camille's wrist. "Nowadays good girls have tattoos?"

"Lust for travelling."

"Meaning?"

"I love wandering the Earth and discovering other lives, other countries, other cultures."

"That's your passion? Like, true passion? Put on special shoes and backpack and wander the earth?"

"Yes."

"And you do it sober, of course?"

"Indeed."

"We toured America, but the real trip was on stage, through music. It was through LSD, through madness, through testing the boundaries of reality, losing control, submerging into chaos. Those were real trips. I've taken LSD so many times, two hundred and fifty, to be exact. And every time it was a real breakthrough. And each time I saw the other side. Real Love. Real Death. Real life, not a superficial Earth-wandering.... And then alcohol, girl. Alcohol. You don't get it, right? Another sip is just another chance. Another chance at bliss."

"Poetic."

"I've always been a poet. But I died a rock-star."

Camille didn't say anything. She was looking at Fred's fingers, hypnotized. As if she could hear the music he was playing.

"And are there other young people like you out there?" Jim asked.

"Quite a lot, actually, yes."

Jim sighed.

"My old man does it too, by the way," Camille said. "He sighs like that when I say that I don't eat meat."

"Fuck your father," Jim frowned, thoughtful.

"You don't have much company at nights here, do you?" Camille asked after a silence, trying to keep calm. "I mean, some young people having a drink at the cemetery at night, you know... Ready to discuss your trips to the other side and other passionate stuff...like death...that kind of thing."

"Much less than before," Jim nodded sadly. "At the beginning they would even take LSD and they also stole the statue from the grave. I was really chuffed. They used to write on graves. They drank themselves unconscious and fell on fences. Now things have changed. Everyone is obsessed with life nowadays. They want long life and order. Rock-n-roll is dead."

"Fucking hell, what a drag!" he repeated, shaking his head.

Camille noticed some people approaching the nearby grave, the one with withering flowers and cigarette ends on it. She looked at her watch. It was ten past eight.

"Our time is up."

"I know," Jim smiled sadly. "Thank you for keeping us company!"

"It was a real pleasure, young lady!" He continued in a deep voice, taking Fred's hand and waving it good-bye.

"Bye, Fred," Camille smiled. "Bye, Jim. And, please, don't..."

But both of them had already disappeared.

Camille stayed there a little longer, lost in her thoughts. Then she ran away, breathing in tender July air and giving her face to soft morning sunlight.

The next day Jim found a bottle of cognac and two fancy glasses hidden behind his grave.